Scoop o'

The deranged Ma[...]
by Kinsey's ear. Kin[...]
ered himself a journalist to the bone, began to
wonder if he had made the right career choice.

Morley backed away from O'Neill and yelled,
"I'm gonna show him. He's a hotshot combat reporter, and he's going to tell the whole world!"

Kinsey swallowed. "What are we going to
tell the world, Major?"

"Come and see." Morley giggled.

"Morley!" O'Neill was making one last try.
"Stop! That's an order!"

"Wormhole activated!" a speaker blared.
"SG-3 returning!"

And then a thunderous roar jerked Kinsey's
attention around.

His mind grasped for words, for some way
to describe what he was seeing. If you took a
giant wave off Maui, funneled it into a cylinder, and whooshed it out with a straw . . .
maybe you would have an image. But it
wasn't water. It was light, or plasma, or something, and it vomited forth from the stone
ring at the top of the ramp. Then *swooshed*
back into itself, but Kinsey couldn't see the
back of the room through the ring anymore.
The plasma settled within the ring like quicksilver covering a mirror. A single thought finally broke through his amazement . . .

"What the *hell* is *that*?"

First Amendment

A STARGATE SG-1™ NOVEL

Ashley McConnell

Based on the story and characters created by
Dean Devlin & Roland Emmerich

Developed for television by
Jonathan Glassner & Brad Wright

A ROC BOOK

ROC
Published by New American Library, a division of
Penguin Putnam Inc., 375 Hudson Street,
New York, New York 10014, U.S.A.
Penguin Books Ltd, 27 Wrights Lane,
London W8 5TZ, England
Penguin Books Australia Ltd, Ringwood,
Victoria, Australia
Penguin Books Canada Ltd, 10 Alcorn Avenue,
Toronto, Ontario, Canada M4V 3B2
Penguin Books (N.Z.) Ltd, 182–190 Wairau Road,
Auckland 10, New Zealand
Penguin Books Ltd, Registered Offices:
Harmondsworth, Middlesex, England

First published by Roc, an imprint of New American Library,
a division of Penguin Putnam Inc.

First Printing, March 2000
10 9 8 7 6 5 4 3 2 1

This book is dedicated

. . . to Ed Cassidy, for whom I had the privilege of working for six years. He's not Canadian, he's not a Brigadier, but he's gleefully Tuckerized herein. Thank you, Ed, for everything . . .

. . . and to SG-1.net, whose comprehensive site helped tremendously in the details. The stuff I got wrong is All My Fault, naturally.

And I'd like to acknowledge tremendous moral support from Dori, Jenn, Jennifer, OzK, and an unbelievably patient meerkat. Thanks, guys.

Author's Note

It should be noted that none of the characters represented as serving as part of NORAD or stationed in the Cheyenne Mountain Complex have any relationship or resemblance whatsoever to those real personnel who actually serve there. In particular, Generals Pace and Cassidy are *entirely* figments of the author's imagination (except of course as noted in the Dedication).

Congress shall make no law respecting an establishment of religion, or prohibiting the free exercise thereof; or abridging the freedom of speech, or of the press; or the right of the people peaceably to assemble, and to petition the government for a redress of grievances.

—First Amendment to the Constitution of the United States of America

"The character of every act depends upon the circumstances in which it is done. The most stringent protection of free speech would not protect a man in falsely shouting "fire" in a theater and causing a panic.

The question in every case is whether the words used are used in such circumstances and are of such a nature as to create a clear and present danger that they will bring about the substantive evils that Congress has a right to prevent."

—Justice Oliver Wendell Holmes, Schenck v. United States (1919)

CHAPTER ONE

Command, George Hammond often thought, just wasn't what it was cracked up to be.

Things were coming through the Gate.

Apophis, wearing the crown of Upper and Lower Egypt, but the uraeus, the Sacred Serpent on his crown, was alive, with venom dripping from its fangs. His eyes glowed, and beams of light flashed from the palms of his avatar's hands, and where the light touched, man and metal melted.

Monsters. Crystals that walked. Giant lizards from Earth's Jurassic past, fangs gaping, saliva dripping. Floods of wormlike larvae that wriggled and hissed and devoured whatever they touched. Poisonous fog the color and consistency of cotton candy, wrapping itself around his people and smothering them where they stood.

And his people, dying of the very air they breathed. Their faces twisting, changing as he watched, foreheads flattening, brow ridges and jaws thickening, becoming coarse. And the running sores and pestilence, at first only tiny disfigurations and barely noticeable marks, but then growing, widening, covering flesh, leaving holes you could see bone through, weeping yellow pus, and nothing could stop them.

His people, fighting.

Fighting the best they knew how, with guns and

explosives and what science they could muster; fighting and dying to defend their site, their nation, their world.

His people were the only ones standing between the horror and the rest of the planet.

Jack O'Neill firing steadily, using one of the Jaffa energy staffs. It was having a marginally better effect on the cotton candy than the Earth weapons were. Teal'C, beside him, using a zat gun.

Janet Frasier was using a Supersoaker to spray antibiotics in a nauseating yellow-green mist.

Daniel Jackson was reading aloud, very seriously, from the Book of the Dead.

Samantha Carter kept yelling, "I'll show you guts!" and kicking a blob of . . . something.

Dozens of others from the various teams were using machine guns, offworld weapons, sticks, clubs, anything at all to defend themselves. They were beating the invasion back, forcing Apophis to reopen the Gate to retreat.

And then they all stopped what they were doing, every one of them, Apophis included, and turned around and looked at *him*, waiting to be told what to do next.

He woke up feeling very annoyed about it.

Most people his age got up on Fridays looking forward to a relaxing weekend, maybe a little golf, some work in the yard, going to church, watching the games. Or at least they were close enough to retirement to think about what a nice day Friday would be, sometime soon. That was nice and normal and made sense.

Of course, in this man's Air Force, that would be tooooo easy. Particularly in this *particular* man's Air Force.

So instead, he got up at 0400 hours and did a brisk couple of miles on the treadmill while watching the latest world crises on CNN, looked over some paperwork, made a few phone calls to Washington, and by the time his driver showed up he had half a day's work done before he'd even gone into the office. You could do that when the house was spacious and empty, and you were the only one rattling around in it.

And besides, keeping busy kept him from thinking about how very quiet the house was. He and Margaret had bought it planning to retire at the end of this last tour of duty: the first house the two of them had ever owned. It was a simple three-bedroom brick ranch style in the suburbs of Colorado Springs, with a swimming pool, drained now for the winter, and a study with all of George's citations and recommendations lovingly framed, and a fireplace they could sit in front of and share a glass of white wine. She'd been so happy with it, planning a garden of perennials, planting trees in the backyard and talking about watching Tessa and Kayla, their granddaughters, climbing them one day.

It was almost like a brand-new start to their marriage, a new beginning after thirty years of transfers from one assignment to the next, ever upward on the promotion ladder. They'd had a daughter who grew up a typical military brat, learning how to blend in to every new situation, knowing that it never lasted long and the next duty station would always be new schools, new friends. When she left to go to college, and then to get married, it was almost as if she'd just had yet another transfer.

But the house in Colorado was going to be the very last time they moved, the very first time they could finally unpack *all* the knicknacks and souvenirs they'd picked up from the tours in Turkey, Germany, England, Japan. Finally, Margaret Hammond could be something other than the perfect officer's lady.

Then the cancer had gotten her. She hadn't even had a chance to see him retire. It had been quick and shocking and even now it hurt terribly to think about.

And of course, once she was gone there was no point in quitting. He wasn't a quitter. He might write a book about all their travels, all his assignments—if only to dedicate it to her.

He tugged the visor of his cap down hard and nodded abruptly to the wedding portrait that graced the front hall. Hard to remember he'd ever been that young. Hard to imagine Margaret had ever been anything other than that beautiful. The train of her wedding gown, a froth of lace, swirled around her feet, and her arm curled around his as she looked up at him, smiling with such incredible happiness, while he looked straight into the camera, awkward and stiff in his second lieutenant's uniform, ridiculously happy too. At the end, frail and bald from chemotherapy and radiation, Margaret still smiled when their daughter came home to help them both through her mother's last days.

Stepping out his front door, he tugged it shut and locked the portrait and the empty house away, and turned his attention to the dark blue sedan pulled up to the curb in front of the house. The neighbor's dog barked sharply, and Hammond nodded to it as well.

The driver, a stolid sergeant who never said anything except "Yes sir," handed him a selection of newspapers and held the door of the staff car for him. Hammond returned the salute and got in, skimming the headlines even as he fastened his seat belt. They were a varied bunch: the *Washington Post*. The *Times* of London. *The Wall Street Journal*. The *Los Angeles Times*. Margaret had enjoyed discussing current events with him, and he'd had to keep sharp to keep up with her. She would have loved his current assignment.

But even if Margaret were still alive he couldn't

have told her anything about his work. He'd rarely been able to. She wouldn't have minded—all career military spouses got used to not knowing things—but he would have, knowing how she would have loved hearing about the wonders, the possibilities that lay so close at hand.

He wouldn't have told her, either, about the threat that lay equally close. Scanning the headlines, absently noting information about the wobbling economy, the latest isolationist edicts from Washington, the threats of terrorism and the anguish of natural disasters, he couldn't find anything at all about the increased activity at Cheyenne Mountain, home of the North American Aerospace Defense Command. That was just fine with him, and it would be just fine with General Austin Pace, Commanding, too.

One of the less wonderful things about Friday was his regular meeting with Austin Pace. Another skirmish in the turf war. Not his favorite thing, though he had to sympathize with the other general. The Mountain was supposed to be Pace's baby, and no commander worth his salt appreciated being saddled with some mysterious black project smack in the middle of his very own base, and then being told he didn't have a high enough clearance or a Need to Know to be briefed on it, but keep those supplies coming and that infrastructure steady, thank you very much. "Project Blue Book." Was anyone really fooled by that?

It was a relatively long drive out to the Mountain from Colorado Springs, through the south end of town and Fort Carson, but at least it hadn't snowed yet. The trees were beginning to turn; aspens were slender white columns crowned with gold, brilliant against the bright-blue mountain sky. There was a snap in the air; there would be snow by the end of the month. Margaret had liked snow, talking about going on sleigh rides like the ones she'd gone on as a child in New Hampshire. Once, before she'd gone, he'd found someone who gave rides, and with the first snow that year he had taken her out, wrapped in yards upon yards of Polarfleece blankets, and they had ridden in the snow behind a pair of big black horses in red harness with jingling bells. She'd had that look again, that incredible happiness as she tried to catch snowflakes on her tongue.

His driver had slowed down, as if to give him a chance to savor the view and the memories, but in truth it was the traffic that was holding them up. As they came off State Road 115 onto NORAD Road, a white van up ahead of them, bristling with antennae, was listing heavily to one side with a flat rear tire; there was no place for it to go on the narrow, curving mountain road. Hammond's sedan jolted as the van veered wildly across the narrow road and then back into its own lane, scraping antennae against pine branches as it did so.

"Sir, please ensure your seat belt is fastened," the sergeant said flatly, slowing down to a crawl. Hammond's eyes narrowed. As they came around one more curve, the road straightened and the shoulder broadened, and the van limped over immediately to take advantage of the room and shudder to a relieved halt. The sedan growled and leaped past, leaving the other vehicle well behind. It looked as if it belonged to the local news media—he caught sight of a local station's logo as they passed.

"Inform the state police that there's a driver in trouble," Hammond said, pleased that his voice was steady. He had been in situations before where a "crippled" van on a remote road could have been real trouble. Ranking American military personnel had been kidnapped and killed by terrorists. Even though this was Colorado, U. S. of A. and definitely not Izmir, Turkey, or Palermo, Italy, the lessons learned about potential ambushes and kidnappings could never be unlearned. A news van had no place on a military reservation, and they were on Fort Carson property here.

He let go a deep breath and thought again, yearningly, about retirement. Once he finally retired, he wouldn't have to worry about such things anymore.

All he'd have to do is stay home and remember.

Active duty was still better than that.

"Yes sir," the sergeant acknowledged. Before he could pick up the car phone, however, it rang, causing both men to jump, then settle back self-consciously.

"Hammond."

The voice at the other end of the line was instantly recognizable as his latest right-hand man, Major Marie Rusalka. Right-hand woman, he amended. Rusalka served as his command team coordinator, and worked remarkably well with his ADC, who was a noncommissioned officer. "General, you asked me to remind you about the tourist briefing scheduled for 1000 hours today."

"Thank you, Major."

As the command center for North American air and space defense, Cheyenne Mountain was a popular destination for visitors, who invariably thought they would get a guided tour of the guts of the mountain, an up-close-and-personal look at the Operations Center, Space Control, Systems, and the other centers of activity that provided surveillance and protection for the U.S. and Canada. The fact that they had to book their visits well in advance probably enhanced their expectations of all the highly technical, highly classified Stuff they were going to get to see.

Invariably, the guests were disappointed to discover that all they were really going to get was a presentation in the Visitors Center. They could have saved themselves the feeling if they'd only read the information handed out ahead of time, or investigated the extensive Website that the Air Force Space Command provided, but no. Every single time someone would stick his hand up in the air and ask the ever-patient officer of the day, "When do we get to go inside and see everything?"

As if, Hammond thought, borrowing one of his granddaughters' favorite phrases.

The blue sedan pulled up at the gatehouse to the complex, and the sentry carefully verified the driver's identity and then the general's, despite having seen them at least four times a week for the past three years. As they passed the Visitors Center, Hammond looked to see if the tourists were already lined up to go inside. It was too early, of course. The Friday morning briefing was always scheduled for 1000 hours, and it was only 0700. The buses wouldn't arrive for at least another three hours.

Satisfied, the sentry waved them through to the next checkpoint.

The sergeant parked the sedan, got the door—it was amazing how fast that man moved, Hammond thought; he *never* managed to beat his driver to opening the door—and escorted the general into the Mountain, where the *real* checkpoints began.

Palm scans, retina scans, visual comparisons. The "Detect" part of the holy Security triad of "Detect Delay Respond" was so much a part of his daily life, and had been for so long, he barely noticed it. He had gone through at least three layers of obvious identification systems (and two more not so obvious) by the time he got to the first set of elevators.

The Mountain had been hollowed out starting in 1961 as the very biggest and best bomb shelter ever. It went fully operational in 1966. All through the Cold War, Cheyenne Mountain had focused intently on the possibility that thermonuclear bombs launched from somewhere in the Communist bloc might rain down on North America. When the sky grew increasingly more crowded with satellites, they kept an eye on those, too, monitoring the other side's spy eyes, tracking the possibility that death might come from space. They continued their job with unrelaxed vigilance when the Cold War was declared "over," well aware that traffic in near space was increasing yearly and that the economic chaos that succeeded the fall of the Berlin Wall had made nuclear weapons available to countries and organizations that previously would have had little chance of obtaining them.

And it wasn't just the U.S. that kept its eyes on the skies. One of the side benefits of having a special relationship with Canada was that the northern country was as deeply involved in NORAD as was the U.S. itself. Command rotated between the two countries. This year it happened to be the U.S. commanding.

The focus for NORAD, always, was on the threat from other countries. It was the responsibility of their highly trained personnel to coordinate the response to any threat to North America coming from within the atmosphere or outside it. It didn't matter whether they believed in a Chinese nuclear threat or little green men from Mars; their job was to Respond and wipe them out of North American skies. Army, Navy, and Air Force Space Command all had a role here.

And none of it was George Hammond's concern.

Hammond passed the first set of elevators, and the second.

He was not accountable to the U.S. Air Force Space Command, or the U.S. Space Command, or NORAD. His name appeared nowhere on their Table of Organization, and he was not in their chain of command. General George Hammond and his personnel had their offices even deeper in the hollowed-out mountain than that. They weren't concerned with the thermonuclear threat or the satellites in near space.

George Hammond commanded the Stargate Complex, and his concerns were literally light-years away from NORAD's and those of NORAD's commanding generals.

Light-years away and far more immediate. Hammond could only imagine how annoyed they'd be to know that the biggest alien threat to North America, or even to the whole planet, wasn't going to appear in the air; it had already materialized twenty-seven stories underneath their feet, in the very deepest guts of Cheyenne Mountain.

And if the tourists at the Visitors' Center had any idea what lay beneath their feet as they sat squirming in hard plastic chairs through the droning hour-and-a-half presentation complete with multimedia show and interactive exhibits, they'd run screaming, he was certain.

CHAPTER TWO

Hammond liked to go first to the briefing room, overlooking the Gate, rather than to his office. His first priority upon arrival at the Complex was reviewing the reports of the various teams currently exploring the worlds of possibility that were accessible through the Gate in the depths of the mountain. In that sense, at least, Hammond's project echoed USSPACECOM; he had Air Force, Army, Navy, and Marine units reporting to him. Hardly anything else was the same.

It saved time to do that initial review in the same room where the team commanders met. The wall of windows looked out over another room, three stories tall, at the far end of which a huge shape, flat and round like a pancake set on end, focused the eye. A shallow steel grid ramp led up to the disk, which consisted of two concentric rings inscribed with alien symbols, surrounding a gleaming iris of overlapping steel plates that completely covered the center. Ramp and disk were set off from the rest of the room by a wide painted border of yellow and black stripes alternating with the legend KEEP CLEAR.

This was the Stargate—the portal to alien worlds, the gateway through which Hammond's teams ventured forth to gather intelligence and possibly find new weapons to fight the Goa'uld, an alien menace that had already visited Earth, taken samples of human populations and cultures, and seeded them on distant worlds for the purpose of harvesting them later as hosts for their larvae.

The rest of the room was taken up with computer consoles and wires and very busy personnel, deciphering signals sent by probes, running programs to try to determine how much the original coordinates of the Gate had been thrown off by galactic drift in the millennia since the Gate was placed on Earth; more busy personnel preparing those probes; and still more trying to keep the computers running instead of crashing from the glut of alien data. And it truly was "alien"—from far more distant stars than NORAD dreamed.

In those early hours, the room was quiet and peaceful, and he always got more done than in his own office. Master Sergeant Harriman, his aide-de-camp, knew Hammond well, and always had a summary and a cup of coffee waiting for him at his place at the end of the long polished table. He settled in to read until his command staff—leaders of the teams on standby, the medical staff, logistics support, and the various analysis teams—showed up.

He had no patience with commanders who made grand entrances when everyone else had already seated themselves. Besides, he liked to see who came in prepared and who had to fumble in briefcases for papers. Harriman, prepared as always, took out copies of all the most current updates to the various reports already supplied, ready to slide them under Hammond's eye as each individual spoke. Shortly thereafter, the rest of his command staff entered and took their places.

There was O'Neill, practically bouncing as he came in. Energy levels too high—the tall colonel needed another mission. He was a good officer but tended to be impatient. "Good morning, sports fans!"

"Morning, Colonel," Harriman acknowledged.

A few of the others, not as inclined to be cheery

in the morning, glared at him. Hammond, remembering his dream, could not prevent a chill from traveling up his spine as he observed them. O'Neill, getting himself coffee from the table in the back, was bantering with some of the other team commanders.

Nearly everyone in the room had been in his dream, he realized. Plus many others who weren't at command level. And they'd all looked at him for direction, just as they did in real life.

Rusalka sat on the other side of him from Harriman. They were both well aware of his little idiosyncracies by this time and had all their ducks in a row. Her tapping of her papers into an obsessively neat, perfectly squared-off pile served to distract him. It had only been a dream, after all. A nightmare. He dismissed the memory.

Assorted other SG commanders, in various stages of readiness, took their places. The Medical staff arrived, looking concerned but not worried, if that distinction could be drawn from across a crowded room. Logistics. Security.

Neither NORAD nor USSPACECOM knew anything at all about the Goa'uld. It was part of Hammond's mission to keep it that way. Putting the briefing room in a position to overlook the Gate served to keep his team's minds firmly on their mission—as if they needed any reminder.

That mission was clearly understood and defined by presidential directive: "to perform reconnaissance, determine threats, and if possible make peaceful contact" with as many worlds as possible. His people, gathering and settling in at their places around the table, were the best of the best from all U.S. military services. They used some of the most powerful computing hardware in the world to calculate the proper sequence of signals to find new Gates and new worlds. Alien worlds.

There was nothing in all of the country, probably

in all of the world, more secret than the work they did right here. These missions were necessary reconnaissance to ensure Earth's survival in an undeclared war against the Goa'uld, a race of parasitic aliens who had borrowed—or stolen—the Gate technology to make travel between worlds easier by opening wormholes between predetermined coordinates. Thousands of years in the past, one of the Goa'uld had set a Gate in ancient Egypt and used it as a base to kidnap humans and seed them all over the galaxy. Now humans used the Gates to try to restore contact with those scattered populations and, to the best of their ability, to find weapons that would enable them to meet the Goa'uld on equal terms.

It wasn't the kind of war that required divisions in the field. It wasn't the kind of war that required propaganda to engage public opinion. It was a desperate, tiny, minute kind of war waged by a handful of men and women who dared not admit to the human race just how dreadful the consequences of failure, of losing, might be.

The first report was always Captain—Dr.—Janet Frasier's. As head of the Medical Department, she had the responsibility to oversee the health of the teams, monitor casualties, and, perhaps most important, to ensure that no one brought back anything insidious or contagious. Warner, her second-in-command, was present at this meeting, somewhat to Hammond's silent relief. Warner was the surgeon, and if he could be spared from the operating theater, it meant that no one needed what they'd come to call, in the gruesome humor typical of people trying to deal with the sometimes unspeakable "body work."

"The bacteria carried back by SG-3 seem to have died off almost immediately," Frasier summarized. "We conclude—provisionally—that the bug is native to M70619, and therefore not well adapted to attack the human species." She slapped the folder shut with something resembling relief. "SG-3 should be ready for return to full duty in less than a week." Putting the first of her manila folders down, she opened the second. "As you are aware, sir, SG-2 suffered severe casualties, but all of those who got back are expected to survive." She frowned at little at the case reports in her hand. "We're seeing some new kinds of injuries, not consistent with earlier experience, and we're wondering if we can get more information on the weapons used. But I emphasize that we do expect recoveries."

There was a little silence, and an ostentatious not-looking at one of the officers seated midway down the table.

"Good news," Hammond nodded, as if there had never been an awkward pause. He went on to the next subject on the agenda automatically, and Frasier sat down again with obvious gratitude.

The morning briefing always followed the same pattern: Frasier's casualty reports and medical updates; reports on which teams were out among the stars; potential new destinations; problem areas; and basic housekeeping. It was one of those reliable things in the universe.

So next Harriman stood up.

"Currently we've got five teams out, Six, Seven, Eight, Nine, and Fourteen. SG-6 and –7 are both on P3X-1492, working on the Tecumseh Codex. They report excellent progress.

"SG-8 is doing some follow-up scientific studies on P5R-221. They still haven't found any sign of human survivors there, but they're not sure whether that's due to climatic changes or if the seed stock they brought with them wasn't able to adjust to the new world. It looks like they managed to last maybe three or four generations before they died out."

Hammond shook his head, wondering how many

worlds had been like twenty-two-one, how many human lives had been wasted by a profligate parasite. *Let them die,* he could imagine the Goa'uld saying. *Earth will make more.*

"Nine hasn't reported back yet. We don't expect to hear from them for another eight to ten hours. We know that there has been recent Goa'uld, or at least Jaffa, activity on Tinkerbelle—er, P3R-620. We aren't sure whether they're coming back or not. The Jaffa, I mean. To P3R." Harriman swallowed, probably hoping he hadn't managed to ill-wish the team.

"SG-14's mission was to destroy a newly discovered Goa'uld hatchery. Initial reports indicate success, but that was six hours ago. We haven't heard anything since."

Janet Frasier sighed and made a note, passing it to her chief surgeon. He nodded grimly.

"Keep me posted on all of them," Hammond said unnecessarily.

"Shouldn't we at least send a follow-up probe on a couple of those?" O'Neill asked.

"We're running out of probes," Harriman responded. "You need to bring them back whenever possible. We can't keep up with the combinations team. They're finding new places to go faster than we can build probes to check them out."

"We've still got people out there—"

Harriman lifted one hand helplessly and turned to the head of the table.

"We'll give them another day, at least. How many new destinations do we have probe reports on?" the general asked, making a command decision to move on.

"Seven," Rusalka responded promptly. "Of those, four don't look like any place we want to visit soon. Three may be possibles." Harriman sat down with relief.

"Oh?" O'Neill challenged. "Who made that determination?" The leader of SG-1 was feeling restless, Hammond could tell. Jack O'Neill didn't like not hearing from teams, and didn't like missions that hadn't gone well. This was a particularly bad day on both counts. As the leader of SG-1, which normally made first contact, he sometimes acted a little proprietary about "his" new worlds. Hammond kept giving him new ones so the colonel wouldn't get in the way of the follow-up teams. O'Neill hadn't been out for a while. It was time to give him fresh meat to chew on, and Rusalka wasn't being very encouraging.

Rusalka shrugged. Part of the duty of the research section of SGC was deciphering new Gate combinations and sending out probes to see what was on the other side before the human teams actually ventured forth. Her group was also responsible for assessing the risk to the first team through. That usually put her in conflict, to one degree or another, with O'Neill.

"Well, we lost three of the four probes immediately, and the fourth one melted in a pool of lava," she responded. "I didn't think you'd want to go wading in that, although it does give new meaning to the concept of a hot tub."

"Well, no wonder we're running out of equipment."

Hammond just barely managed to keep from rolling his eyes in exasperation. He couldn't keep O'Neill from making wisecracks, he'd realized long ago, and he couldn't keep Rusalka from trying to set him down a notch. He wondered if Rusalka considered the colonel a challenge of some kind. Maybe he should ask Frasier to have a little woman-to-woman talk with the major. Maybe get Sam Carter into it, too.

For an instant he toyed with the idea of asking Carter to set up a formal female-only staff briefing on How to Handle O'Neill, but it would be useless anyway. Incorrigible.

Besides, they were adults and they'd damn well work it out on their own time. Or else.

Incorrigible took up the report. "The rest of our teams are twiddling their thumbs, ready to go," O'Neill said. "SG-1 is more than ready for its next assignment—as soon as we can find someplace other than a lava pool to dip our toes in."

"We still have three possibles," Rusalka continued grimly as though she hadn't been interrupted, "although I don't like the atmospheric readings on two of them. We haven't finished interpreting the data."

"Standing by."

"If you really want to use total environmental suits for your next mission, my team should have a report by the time we finish up here, Colonel. If you'd care to stop by the labs we'll have the lists for you."

O'Neill grunted and waved his hand as if to say, *I'll wait*.

The reports went on, a smooth flow of information, comments, suggestions, decisions. Hammond orchestrated it all, watching as his command team worked together, letting them sort through options, goals, plans. They were good at what they did.

Usually.

But every once in a while, things went rather horribly wrong, and they weren't able to blame the Goa'uld.

CHAPTER THREE

"I'd like to hear now from SG-2 about the details of their last mission," Hammond said at last. "I believe that's the world you called Etaa, Jack."

"That's what the inhabitants called their city, yes."

The officers around the table looked at each other uncomfortably, then directed their gazes to the major sitting halfway between Hammond and O'Neill.

"Major Morley?" Hammond prompted, his voice oddly gentle.

Morley cleared his throat and looked down at the papers carefully squared on the table in front of him. His face was heavily bruised along the left side, the entire left eye surrounded by black markings; a pattern of stitches along the cheekbone held together a raw gash. When he moved his arm along the table it was clear that he was favoring it. The end of a bandage peeked out from under the cuff of his jacket.

When no one broke the silence, he sighed, sharply catching his breath halfway through the exhalation. "Yes, sir."

Without looking up, he continued, pitching his voice just loud enough to be heard clearly by all those at the table, "As you are aware, sir, our assignment was the recovery of SG-4 personnel captured by the Goa'uld on P7X-924."

Piece of cake, Morley thought, as his squad formed up for one last weapons check before going through the Gate.

He hadn't actually been to P7X-924 before, but he'd spent hours poring over the probe reports. He knew everything there was to know about the Goa'uld, everything that had ever been reported by O'Neill and his hotshot team. This was going to show just how good he really was. That downcheck on his last evaluation would be wiped away as if it had never happened. Hammond would see that O'Neill just didn't want the competition, didn't want anybody who could maybe take his place one day as the leader of SG-1. O'Neill had told the boss that Morley was the wrong choice, he had no experience.

The hell he didn't. Maybe he'd never been through the Gate before, but he'd been on plenty of recoveries on Earth. It wasn't any different just because the sky was a different color. And he deserved the chance. What happened last time, in Iraq, well, that wasn't his fault, and anybody who wanted to give him a fair shake knew it. The temporary vacancy in the command position for SG-2 was a godsend.

He'd argued long and hard for this assignment, and it was all going to go perfectly. Perfectly. Hammond thought so too, or he wouldn't have let Morley go.

The reports all said that the wormhole was cold. At first he'd figured that was just more bull—making it look harder than it was. But it had come up again and again, in all the reports from all the teams.

And whaddaya know, they were right. Damn. For those long minutes—or was it only seconds? Impossible to tell— he was frozen right down to his guts. He hoped he still had his weapon—all his weapons. Couldn't feel anything.

But then they'd come out the other side, and for the first time ever, Morley was on an alien world.

The first thing he did, as soon as he could feel anything, was spin around and count his men to make sure they'd all come through okay, make sure the F.R.E.D. with all their weapons and supplies was there. And the DHD. Had to make sure they weren't trapped. Of course, there had been at least two teams through this Gate already, and the very first probe had verified, but it never hurt to check.

O'Neill had gotten caught that way; it wasn't going to happen to him.

Yeah, all twenty of them present and accounted for. And there was the DHD. It looked just as they described it in the reports, a wide round platform with squares marked by the Goa'uld coordinate symbols, with a big red dome in the middle, the whole thing standing about a yard high and a yard wide, including the base column. The face was angled to allow easy access to the thirty-nine glyphs that surrounded the activating dome.

That took care of the first two things. The third was detecting the presence of hostiles. He could afford to make that number three in his hit parade because he had recent intelligence from the probe. Sure enough, the area around the Gate was quiet.

And then he could afford to take a deep breath of the alien air of an alien world.

It smelled funny. Like a bowl full of nuts.

The air was the wrong color, too. Well, not that air could have color, really, but the sky was a peculiar reddish blue, and he had the feeling he was looking at things through pink-violet-tinted lenses. At least it was warm, much warmer than the wormhole; he could feel his face tingling in response to the higher temperature. His men were looking around, blinking, trying to adjust, and stumbling their first few steps in a new and heavier gravity. One point two times Earth, the report had said. Morley had trained with extra weights to prepare for it.

But none of that mattered. He'd told Hammond that, and he believed it. What mattered was the mission.

"Okay, let's move out!" His voice sounded different in this air, too, but that was something else that didn't matter. His men responded exactly as they were trained.

Four members of SG-4 had made it back from P7X-924. They said they'd lost fourteen more in a pitched battle with Jaffa and natives. There were still at least three men, last seen being dragged into a native stronghold, whose current status was unknown. That was the same native stronghold that O'Neill had rhapsodized about being so friendly and cooperative. Hah.

SG-1 had made first contact with this world and came back with the message that all was well, the people of this world were ready and eager to cooperate with Earth in the battle against their common enemy. So when SG-4 had gone in with a full research team, they'd expected to find allies, not a trap. They were easy pickings. O'Neill felt guilty about it, of course—he'd screwed up royally, not that anybody would ever admit it. That was another reason why O'Neill had tried to take over this assignment. But it was SG-2's job to do the dirty work, and they were here to do it. Under a competent commander, dammit.

The area around the Gate was cleared ground. The few patches of trees nearby were at least twenty yards away. SG-2 hustled for cover, taking its bearing from the directions they'd been given; on the other side of that line of vegetation, there'd be a broad plain, and then the tall towers that marked the native stronghold.

The natives were strictly low tech, the reports said. The only thing they'd have to worry about was the Jaffa. But those reports were from SG-1, and Morley wasn't dumb enough to believe them, even though the survivors agreed that the only heavy artillery belonged to the Jaffa. He moved his men through dripping trees and oily vines, ignoring the shrieks of things that probably weren't birds.

His second-in-command, Lieutenant Fries, kept looking up, as if trying to identify the noises. Alarm calls? Morley wondered. But no, it couldn't be. There was so much noise, coming from all directions, that nobody could tell if one particular set of shrill cries was a warning of intruders.

They formed a loose array at the tree line, grenade launchers already loaded and ready. The tactical meeting had discussed the possibility of a direct frontal attack: "Let's blow a hole in it and blast them to hell and back."

Unfortunately that would probably result in the immediate deaths of the captives, so that plan was discarded, somewhat to Morley's disappointment.

There had been speculation about whether the captives were still alive or even still on P7X-924. Morley refused to call it Etaa—that was just another instance of O'Neill losing sight of the mission. So what if that's what the natives called home? The man had to personalize everything. Planetary coordinate designation numbers were good enough for Morley. It wasn't like he was planning a vacation here.

The behavior of the Jaffa and their efforts to capture some of the SG-4 team alive argued that the humans had been taken for a reason, probably interrogation. Hammond had decreed that SG-2 would assume the captives were alive unless otherwise proven. As for their location, well, if they weren't still on the purple world, it would be up to SG-2 to find out where they'd been taken.

The town looked pretty much as described—mud walls, two big circular stone towers on either side of a pair of outsize wooden gates bound by rough iron. The place was the biggest "city" identified so far on this planet, and it only had a population of maybe ten thousand or so. Some outlying farms existed, but nobody had investigated them yet. SG-1 had said there was a lot of movement in and out of Etaa-the-city, but right now the gates gaped open and empty.

No activity in the streets of the city was visible through the gate. Fries looked over at Morley and shrugged, a half-grin on his face. "Quiet," he whispered. "Too quiet."

It was, of course. There should have been activity. The Gate was close enough to the main population center that its activation wouldn't have gone unnoticed.

"Launch a spy eye," Morley had ordered. Fries had to dig the little remote-controlled plane out of his pack, set it up.

And then the enemy had opened fire.

The humans had retreated and scattered along the tree line, hitting the ground and returning fire. High explosives roared. Lances of pure energy pierced the trees.

If the other side had been human, Morley would have

expected them to use infrared to locate and target the body heat of intruders. Infrared, of course, worked best at night, when the blurring effect of the heat of the sun was absent.

They were not human. It wasn't clear exactly what weapon they were using—probably those damned energy staffs—but at least the humans could tell where the most accurate blasts were coming from. Fire from seven grenade launchers converged on a single point in the long, skinny window of the tallest tower.

The tower blew apart.

The bird things weren't making noise anymore, Morley noted absently.

The frequency of hostile fire was substantially lessened. Morley signaled his men to spread out in an even longer line, making them a more difficult target. As they did so, every other member of the team stopped firing. Or at least, it was supposed to be every other member of the team; there seemed to be holes in the line.

There was activity at last around the base of the ruined tower. Morley could see several natives and one or two serpent-headed Jaffa ducking in and out between the rubble and toppled stone blocks. Fries, a highly trained sniper, took one of the Goa'uld troops out with one of the new, specially formulated explosive bullets, designed to punch through Jaffa armor like copkillers through Teflon. If there really had been a second Jaffa, he was smart enough to keep his head down. There was a scraping sound, loud enough in a sudden silence to hurt the eardrums, and then nothing but drifting smoke.

Piece of cake, Morley thought deliriously. If the Jaffa were still here, the prisoners were probably here too. All they had to do was take out the Goa'uld servants, walk in, and walk out again.

The line began cautiously moving forward under cover of the smoke and dust from the exploded tower. They could see strange objects weaving back and forth—Goa'uld machines? SG-2 kept firing, alternating between odd and even members of the line, laying down cover for themselves. There were no return energy blasts, though a few slender, arrowlike wands bounced harmlessly off their helmets and body armor. With growing confidence, they moved up to the city wall.

Morley looked around to assess his casualties. At least four were missing. He'd pick them up on the way back, he promised himself. He wasn't leaving any humans on this planet, dead or alive.

The battle line began to contract as they approached the open gate. "Sir!" Fries called his attention to an opening in the remains of the blasted tower. "Look! There's someone up there!"

There was. He could see a shadow, and on some instinct he ordered his men to hold their fire. That instinct was rewarded as he glimpsed a distinct pattern of jungle camouflage.

"They're up there!" He was going to do it. He'd taught those damned Jaffa, and those traitorous natives took a lesson—they couldn't just grab Earth humans and think they could get away with it.

He left three men at the foot of the ruined tower to guard their backs, and led the rest inside. Even if they'd cleaned out the Jaffa, there were still those natives, after all. Though they represented no threat at all.

"There was some kind of force field waiting for us," he said, the words difficult to force past his dry throat. "At the top of the stairs they had the bodies of the remaining members of SG-4 propped up as if they were standing there waiting for us. And the rest of the Jaffa were standing on either side."

The rest of the Jaffa . . . as if they were standing there waiting for us.

And what was waiting behind them—

Morley shook his head, hard, blocking the picture out of his mind.

Someone pushed a carafe of water and a glass toward him, and he poured unsteadily, one container rattling against the other as he did so. The water was cool against the lining of his throat.

"Any ideas about the nature or source of the force field?" It was O'Neill, his voice carefully lacking in accusation or judgment. It might have been a question asked for the mere curiosity of it, except for the underlying intensity.

Morley put the glass down and shook his head. "I don't know. I thought, thought maybe it was a Goa'uld we hadn't seen, using those, those *powers* of theirs."

No one reminded him of his own remarks of only a week before, scorning the reports of "bug-eyed aliens with mental zap guns."

No one had to.

"But we didn't see one," he forced himself to go on, still not looking up. "All we saw were . . . Jaffa. There were at least a dozen of them, and we were fish in a barrel. They got Paul Fries with the first volley."

All we saw were . . . Jaffa . . .

A pin dropping on the wooden table, bouncing, would have made more noise than his audience.

"Most of us got knocked out. When we woke up, they had us locked up in this big square stone room. It was still daylight, we could tell from the windows up near the ceiling.

"And then they came and started taking us away to ask us . . . questions." His hands were clasping each other now, the knuckles white and red from the desperation of his grip. "I thought, I thought they'd be tactical stuff. You know, like whether there were more of us, and what weapons—" He lifted his gaze from its fixed study of his trembling hands, finally, and looked around at them, his mouth working, no words coming out.

Hammond shot a sharp look at Frasier. She was watching Morley very carefully, clearly worried but

· not yet ready to call a halt to a briefing that had turned, despite the general's best intentions, into a public confession.

"They didn't care. They didn't *care*. They were just laughing at us. It was as if we couldn't possibly threaten them. Nothing Earth could do could threaten the . . . Goa'uld." *It was laughter. Had to be.*

He paused again, and something changed behind his eyes. "They roughed up some of the boys, but not too bad." It was clear that he wasn't thinking about his own injuries. "When they sent me back into that room, we decided we weren't going to wait any longer. They didn't come for any more of us until the next morning, and then when they did, we, we rushed them." *Didn't we?*

"There were only two"—*weren't there?*—"a-and we got past them." He swallowed hard. "Most of us did. Sergeant Wilkinson and Captain Dell'angelo both had broken legs. They were still up in the, the tower. We tried to take them with us but—" *but it was too late—*

"That's enough, Major." Hammond spoke quietly. "You managed to get the remainder of your squad back home. You had no reason to suspect a trap."

He could sense O'Neill's disagreement from the opposite end of the table, but that wasn't the issue and he wasn't going to open the matter up for debate in this forum. The mission had been a spectacular failure; not only had it failed of its objective, the retrieval of the captives, but more than half of the "rescue" squad had been lost as well. Including the abandonment of two men. They were back where they'd started—farther behind where they'd started, in fact, counting all the dead.

He wasn't going to order yet another team in to try to recover the two men. It made his teeth ache to bite that order back, but P7X-924 was bad luck and an asset sink as well. They would have to assume

Wilkinson and Dell'angelo were dead—probably as soon as the rest of SG-2 had operated the Gate for their return home. The Jaffa would have killed them just as they'd killed the "survivors" of SG-4. They were injured and of no tactical use. There was no interstellar Red Cross to parley for an exchange of prisoners in this war.

It was time to move on to the final item on the agenda. He'd give the problem of David Morley and Etaa further consideration—it deserved investigation—but not here, not now.

"Harriman? I need to be able to tell Pace that we've scoped out the costs for repairing the damage our little vibration problem—our *former* vibration problem—caused." When Cheyenne Mountain had been built originally, they'd had a small problem with a geological fault in the mountain. When they first started operating the Gate on a regular basis, the alien artifact had shaken the entire mountain. The problem had been solved, but someone had to pay for the repairs to all the other facilities affected.

Davis, the man in charge of Gate operations and maintenance, stood up. He seemed to be as eager as the rest to change the subject, to direct attention away from the officer who stared now at his hands, oblivious to anything else going on around him. "Er, sir, I have the data, but some of the other analyses don't quite agree. They, er, the others, keep finding a lot of, well, they call it collateral damage."

"Hmmph." Hammond took the printout and scanned it quickly. There were always those gray areas where damage could be attributed to more than one cause. "I take it that if we accept responsibility for this list, the repairs and replacements come out of *our* budget?"

"Yes, sir."

"Hmmph," Hammond repeated. "I have a meeting with Pace later today. I'll talk to him about it. We don't need to run up our costs any more than he does." And certain senators were far less likely to pick on NORAD than SGC when it came to costs.

"In fact, sir," Rusalka interjected, "I'd appreciate it if you could also speak to General Pace about the procurement lists for medical supplies and parts for the probes. They go through his offices, and some of his personnel have been questioning our needs."

"Tsk, tsk," O'Neill, commanding SG-1, remarked. "You mean they think something funny's going on down here?"

"Possibly the excessive requirements for antibiotics attracted their attention," Rusalka parried, with a straight face.

"You mean we've been using too much penicillin? Gee, I thought we'd cured that little problem."

"That will be enough," Hammond said. "Harriman, add it to the list. They've got no business questioning anything that comes through here."

"That's probably what ticks them off," O'Neill muttered.

The other team commanders, four out of the fourteen, chuckled. Hammond cleared his throat. O'Neill and the rest immediately assumed looks of angelic innocence, perfected by long practice.

The morning briefing wound down to a close, and the assembled officers rose and gathered their papers, exchanging a few last comments as they went. O'Neill paused, drawing breath to speak to his commander, and then shook his head and went away, rather to Hammond's relief.

Harriman stood respectfully by, agenda in hand.

"All right, what's next?" Hammond muttered.

"Short break, sir, and then the meeting with General Pace."

Hammond sighed inaudibly. Meetings. Decisions. Command was *not* all it was cracked up to be.

CHAPTER FOUR

"So what's the good word, Colonel?" Sam Carter was feeling almost jaunty. She'd just managed to destroy Daniel Jackson in a fast game of racquetball, and now, having showered and gotten into clean, if casual, clothes, she was ready to take on the world. Or possibly the worlds, depending on what the next assignment was.

But as soon as the words were out of her mouth she regretted them, having caught sight of O'Neill's face. He looked grim, to put it mildly.

"I'm not sure there *is* a good word today," the colonel growled.

"Uh-oh," Jackson observed. "What happened?"

"Is it something to do with the members of SG-2 presently in Medical?" asked Teal'C.

The team members of SG-1 were gathered in O'Neill's office, their informal ready room for post-command-meeting briefings. It wasn't unusual for O'Neill to come away from one of those briefings annoyed or exasperated, but this time he looked frustrated as well as angry. He was standing with his back to them, staring at the giant poster of stars that covered his back wall. A scattering of pushpins marked places they'd been, or might have been, as closely as they could correlate the outdated star map with the reality of the Gate.

"What do you know about SG-2?" the colonel asked Teal'C, finally turning to face them.

Someone else might have been intimidated, but nothing and no one intimidated the former Jaffa First, who had left the service of Apophis in the hope that one day he could find a way for his people to be free. Certainly O'Neill couldn't do it—they had saved each other's life too many times.

"I was providing more blood specimens to Dr. Frasier," the black man said. "She is still examining the symbiotic relationship between the Goa'uld larva and my body."

O'Neill winced involuntarily, as he did most times when he was reminded of the creature that lived in Teal'C's abdomen.

"I observed the arrival of several injured personnel. Upon inquiry they proved to be members of SG-2. I believe that team had attempted a retrieval on P7X-924. They did not appear to have been successful."

"They weren't," O'Neill responded, leaning against his desk and folding his arms across his chest. "They walked into a trap. Not only did they not get the guys they were sent for, they lost a bunch of their own."

"Oh," Carter said in a very small voice. She knew—they all knew—how much Jack O'Neill hated the very thought of leaving someone behind in the hands of the enemy. Perhaps because SG-1 depended profoundly on one another and the trust that they'd never abandon one of their own.

That trust had been tested and forged in battle. There had been occasions when one or another of them, separated from the others, had had to depend on it for life itself. They had come to accept that it could not be broken, not by outside forces or even by themselves.

But for Jack O'Neill, the issue had nothing to do with trust and everything to do with responsibility.

"Morley ran into a trap," he said angrily. "They used some kind of force field on the team, he says. But he managed to break free and get at least some of his guys back."

"But not all of them," Jackson said softly.

"No. Not all of them."

"What about SG-4?" Carter asked, recalling the group SG-2 had been sent after.

"All dead, apparently."

She closed her eyes and took a deep breath.

"There may indeed be a type of force field available to the Jaffa," Teal'C said thoughtfully. "Such a device was being developed. It may have been perfected by now."

"I don't understand how we could have been so wrong about Etaa," Carter said. "I thought Shosto-ka'an was being straight with us. She said they'd never encountered the Jaffa."

"It is possible they had not," Teal'C reminded her. "The Goa'uld could have decided only recently to harvest that world."

There was a small silence at his choice of words.

"I don't know," O'Neill said. "I don't like the whole story. It just doesn't sound right. There's just something screwy about it, and I can't put my finger on it." The colonel was profoundly dissatisfied.

"Etaa doesn't deserve to be just abandoned," Jackson said. "Those are still human beings there."

"*If* there are still human beings there," Carter pointed out. "It sounds like they were pretty thoroughly cleaned out."

Uncomfortable, Jackson changed the subject. "What about our next mission?" It felt strange, not being able to find the right words to mourn dead comrades, focusing instead on their own upcoming assignment. The archaeologist wondered if O'Neill's pragmatism was catching.

O'Neill cheered up slightly at the prospect of a new world. "Rusalka says she's got something, maybe, but no details yet. The one we thought we had turns out to be in the middle of a volcano or something."

"Nothing like a little pyroclastic flow to get your juices going."

O'Neill glared at him. "Daniel, you're stealing my lines. I've told you about that before."

The archaeologist shrugged. "I told her we weren't going to use that Gate as soon as I saw the probe data. I'm just surprised it hasn't been buried under tons of molten mud by now."

Carter glanced at Teal'C, who was observing the byplay with his customary lack of expression. While O'Neill and Jackson might displace their grief, at least publicly, about the loss of colleagues with sharp-edged banter about volcanoes, Teal'C remained silent, as if the well-defined muscles of his face were set in stone. The only sign of emotional connection the Jaffa had made to the discussion of the dead was a momentary closing of his massive hand when he mentioned the development of the force field. That would have been a reference to the days when Teal'C was Jaffa First to Apophis, Lord of the Goa'uld and deadly enemy to all that was human.

"So she's still looking for a good set of coordinates?" Carter asked. It felt like an inane effort to keep the conversation going, to add to the discussion, but it served its purpose.

"She said she thought she had something," O'Neill admitted. "I suppose we'd better be ready to get together and look at the probe data." He pushed himself away from the desk and circled behind it to sit in the swivel chair. "Look, I've got some paperwork to do, and I'm sure you all have full social calendars too. I'll page you if something comes up."

"So they're just going to forget Etaa? That's not right. Those people might still be alive." Jackson was surprised, sometimes, by how firmly he identified with the whole of Stargate Command.

"No, Daniel, we're not," O'Neill said evenly. "But we're not going to do anything about it right now. I don't like it any better than anybody else, but that's the decision."

The archaeologist sighed and followed the other two out of the office, leaving a discontented colonel behind, staring at the poster showing the field of stars.

Austin Pace, CinC Cheyenne Mountain Operations Center, was a medium man: medium height, medium weight, medium gray hair. He'd been a pilot, served in Nam and the Gulf War, had a chestful of decorations that he usually didn't bother with. He commanded both NORAD and USSPACECOM, the heart of U.S. and Canadian air and space defenses. His first appointment of the day, Brigadier Ed Cassidy, was his deputy commander in chief for NORAD and represented the interests of the Canadian government. Cassidy was always the first person he saw every day, and the last.

"Understand we're having some visitors today," Cassidy said, pouring himself a cup of coffee.

"We always have visitors on Friday."

Cassidy smiled, added milk to his coffee, and sat down. "The Visitors Center always has visitors on Friday, Austin." He patted gently at the neat gray mustache that trimmed his upper lip. "But *we* hardly ever do. Wonderful coffee you get here."

"They're from the Senate office, Ed. We'll just shoo them in and out again." Pace leaned back in his swivel chair. Unlike the offices in the lower sections of the complex, the commander's office was paneled in softly burnished medium-light maple. An American flag, and a Canadian flag flanked the NORAD logo that graced the wall behind his impressively large desk, also in maple. The floor was carpeted in a businesslike blue that was vacuumed every night. A circular table, surrounded by comfortable chairs, served for conferences. At the moment it held a rather nice tea service, a coffeepot, and a covered plate of scones. Pace got up and removed the cloth, inspecting the offerings.

"Oh, naturally. I'm not objecting, of course. You were quite decent about all the disruption last year with HRH's visit. One does rather wonder, though, how our shaky friends downstairs will like the idea." Cassidy carefully brushed a bit of pastry out of his mustache.

"They won't like it at all, but it isn't their problem. The visitors will never get that far."

"No, of course not. But you're going to tell them?"

"Yes, of course. This morning." Restless, Pace moved away from the table and stalked behind his desk, shoving a precisely aligned telephone out of the way to get to the keyboard of his computer terminal.

"George isn't going to be happy about it," Cassidy observed. "Kinsey—he's been here before, hasn't he?"

"No, that was his father."

"So not the senator himself."

"No, thank God."

Cassidy drained his coffee cup and set it down gently with every evidence of satisfaction. "Well, it's your worry, Austin. I myself plan to be fully occupied with the upgrade of the Survivable Communications Integration System. I'll let you worry about actually surviving your communications with your Blue Book fellow."

Pace snorted, bringing a document up on the

screen. "Thank you for the fraternal cooperation of Her Majesty's Commonwealth of Canada."

Cassidy chuckled. "Any time, old man. Come to think of it, perhaps I'll stay and watch. You Americans always have such interesting fireworks displays."

"Hammond doesn't have anything to worry about," Pace repeated irritably. "I'm having my staff notify his. No surprises."

"No, of course not. Never any surprises around here."

Marie Rusalka shared an office with Devorah Randolph, O'Neill's logistics officer. The two of them also shared recipes, child care tips, and the occasional wicked speculation about various members of Hammond's command team. It was a convenient arrangement, because Rusalka's analysis of probe data provided Randolph with a head start on assembling the most likely support that SG-1 would need on each new mission. Rusalka's desk was covered with computer components; Randolph's was covered with lists.

The probe data came back in sound, pictures, and line after line of electronic code, providing reams of environmental data. Sometimes the data flow was abruptly terminated, leaving Rusalka with just enough information to determine that the hapless machine had toppled out of the destination Stargate and splashed directly into a pool of molten lava, or that it had been almost instantly destroyed by hostile activity. Those were, she admitted to herself, the ones she liked best, because puzzling out what had happened in the few seconds' worth of transmission was a lot like solving a crossword puzzle: filling in bits and pieces here and there until suddenly what had been a large gap in their information became a solid, or mostly solid, conclusion.

She was hunched over one of those gaps, her lips moving silently as she considered and rejected possible explanations, when Randolph came in and flung herself into her chair, spinning around to glare at the bulletin board fixed to the wall behind her desk.

Attached to the board were various official pronouncements, Orders of the Day, schedules, and pictures of her six-year-old identical twin girls. "I am supposed to throw a birthday party," she announced grimly. "At school. They want home-baked cookies for thirty. On a Saturday!"

"Furr's," Rusalka said absently, naming a local grocery store.

Randolph spun around and began digging through the papers that covered her desk like the aftermath of a pulp avalanche. "Well, of course Furr's. C-4, environmental—no, wrong one, although come to think of it those environmental suits might come in handy—have you ever tried cleaning up after thirty six-year-olds? Napkins—oh, here it is—and party hats, and noise-makers—why on *earth* do they think six-year-olds need to make *more* noise?—and spoons—why couldn't they have given me more lead time . . ."

"You've got a whole day. Who's doing the punch?" Rusalka still hadn't looked up.

"Not me. I draw the line at punch. I ought to make Jesse do all this stuff. *He* doesn't have to stick to eight-till-whenever."

Jesse Randolph was a farrier. He was perfectly happy to follow his wife from duty assignment to duty assignment, able to find work anywhere there were horses to shoe. The only time they'd ever had problems with career conflicts was Devorah's tour on Kwadjalein Island, and that had only lasted thirty months. It had also resulted in the birth of the twins. Randolph made sure there were horses at their next duty station. It was very important to keep her husband occupied. And tired.

"So tell him to do it." Rusalka was single. She kept goldfish, unsuccessfully.

"No, I should do it. Be Mom for a change." Randolph sighed, spun around again in a 360-degree circle to end up facing her colleague, and changed the subject to something she obviously considered much more pleasant. "Sometimes I lose track of who I am, you know? Mom at home, supersecret support here. I can't decide which role deserves the superhero costume." She brandished an imaginary cape. "So whaddaya have? Anything good?"

"Just what I was wondering myself." The two women looked up to see Jack O'Neill standing in the doorway. "I vote for SuperMom, by the way; you've already got a costume for this job." He shifted his attention to Rusalka. "You mentioned some possibles in the briefing."

Reluctantly, Rusalka pulled her attention away from her beloved data and nodded to her superior officer. O'Neill entered the room, claimed the one visitor's chair that was normally wedged between the two desks, and sat down, sprawling, his long legs effectively taking up the rest of the room between the desks. "Well?" he prompted. "You said you had three possibles."

"We're still evaluating," she said with an air of protest. "The air looks crappy, I said so in the briefing."

"Well, since Harriman thinks we've hit a snag on deciphering coordinates, *and* we're running low on probes, we'd better get *something* out of it." He raised his eyebrows expectantly.

"You really *like* this job, don't you?" Rusalka groused. "Okay, okay. One probe is just transmitting dark. Some of the research department think it's in a cave or possibly underground. It's still operating, but we're just not getting anything. That's one of the bad-air ones."

"Maybe somebody threw a rug over it."

Rusalka gave him a Look. He returned it blandly.

"We have another probe that's transmitting steadily, but it seems to be in the middle of—" She hesitated, as if reluctant to put the concept into words. "It looks like all hell broke out all around it. There seems to be a pitched battle going on."

"And nobody's plastered it yet?"

"I don't think anybody's even noticed the Gate activated," she said, shaking her head, "much less one Earth probe. I keep expecting it to go splat. But so far it's operating perfectly."

"Have you gotten a look at the combatants? Are they Goa'uld?"

"We have no idea. All we see is dust and explosions. All we hear is noise—we had to turn down the volume on it, and the techs are trying to separate out the inputs but so far haven't had any luck."

"Where is it? I want to take a look at it." O'Neill pulled himself up, got up and turned the chair around, sitting in it backward. It made a little more room in the room, at least.

Rusalka gave him an exasperated look. "It's in the lab. We're still working on it, trying to get better resolution, to see if we can actually *see* anything on it yet."

"Oh." O'Neill was disappointed but not discouraged. "And the third probe?"

"The third probe doesn't show any sign of human life anywhere." She bit her lip. "At least, no surviving human life. I don't think people *can* survive there. The atmosphere seems to be mostly methane."

Stepping over to a projector, she touched a control. Lights automatically dimmed as an image was thrown against a white wall. It shuddered and jerked, presumably as the probe rolled out of the Gate and over a few rocks, and then was still.

Nothing moved anywhere on the landscape that the probe surveyed. The ground was charred gray and black, as if it had once been a velvety landscape that was then hit by a solar flare. The horizon faded into a dull gray in the distance. Nowhere within the scope of the probe's lens were any signs of trees, buildings, or even crumbled walls. Just rocks and uneven ground and ash.

"Ick," O'Neill remarked comprehensively. "That's it?"

"Pretty much," Rusalka said. "We think the probe got stuck, because it hasn't moved from that point. This world is very Earth-like as far as gravity goes, but the ground is rock and ash. We haven't seen any sign of indigenous life—animals, birds, or even any insects."

"Radiation?"

"No. We don't know what caused this, or how far it extends. It could be Paradise just outside the range of the lens, but considering how still it is, I wouldn't bet on it."

"Hmmm." O'Neill was silent for a moment. Then: "Which one would you recommend we tackle, Major?"

"Right now, none of them," she responded promptly. "We plan to send a really *big* flashlight through to the first of the three worlds, see if we can light up the place a bit. The probe has just been rolling around randomly, bumping into things and changing directions. We have no idea at all what's there.

"The second location looks like just an all-round bad idea.

"And I'd like to see if anything changes on the third one before anybody goes charging in there."

"Recommendations noted." O'Neill got up and waved a casual salute. "Thanks. 'Ah'll be bahck.' "

The two women rolled their eyes as he left.

"How much you want to bet he goes for Door Number Two?" Randolph asked, reaching for a scrap of paper to start a new list.

"Are you suggesting our beloved colonel likes to go out looking for fights?"

"I'm suggesting our beloved colonel is bored out of his mind. He hasn't been anywhere for at least a couple of weeks. He likes Adventures."

"Nasty things, make you late for dinner."

"I wish I could go," Randolph said wistfully. "It must be so . . . *awesome*, going to new worlds and stuff."

"Yeah? You looked at the casualty lists lately?" Rusalka had very strong and very practical views on the whole starhopping issue. "What would you do with your girls? I'll stay right where I am, thanks. And hope they don't let anything follow them home. It might want to keep us."

The gray phone on Major Rusalka's desk rang then, and both women jumped. With one eyebrow hiked high, Rusalka picked up the receiver. Randolph watched with growing curiosity as the major made noncommittal noises, scratched a neat reminder on a memo pad, and finally hung up the phone. Her face was several shades paler than when she'd begun the conversation. She stared at the instrument, her hand on the receiver, for so long that Randolph thought she was going to burst.

"Well? *What?*"

"Oooooh, shit." Rusalka's hand finally fell away from the receiver, but she continued staring at it for a moment longer, as if it had suddenly turned into something poisonous.

"What is it?" Devorah had never heard her office

mate use an expletive in the entire time they'd shared space. "What's wrong?"

"You know those visitors they're having today?" Rusalka said, pronouncing the words with difficulty. "Well, it turns out that one of them is a reporter."

"So?"

"He's Frank Kinsey. Senator Kinsey's son. You remember Senator Kinsey?"

"*Oh.*" Everyone at SGC remembered, with shudders, the last visit from Senator Lyle Kinsey, who had come within a hairsbreadth of shutting down the project completely. "The general is not gonna like this," she predicted somberly.

"Yeah, and guess who gets to tell him?" Rusalka muttered. She threw the other woman a salute with one hand as she picked up the receiver again with the other. "We who are about to die . . ."

"*You* die. *I'm* going to pull up everything I can find on the guy," Randolph muttered, spinning her chair once again to stop in front of her computer keyboard.

CHAPTER FIVE

Hammond's lips tightened, and his knuckles went white around the receiver. "Understood, Major." He disconnected and scowled.

Senator Kinsey had nearly pulled the rug out from under him once before. It couldn't be a coincidence that his son was snooping around, no doubt looking for a story. The "public" face of the Complex did provide the occasional tour for the interested (and usually high-ranking) civilian, but it was always scheduled well in advance and Pace made sure that Hammond was fully informed. Hitting him out of the blue this way was a violation of their agreement: Pace provided cover and no nasty surprises, and Hammond provided . . . no nasty surprises. The difference was that Hammond pretty much knew exactly what kind of surprises Pace could come up with, while Pace had absolutely no idea what he was being sheltered from. It was another reason Pace didn't like the arrangement.

Barely hesitating, Hammond got up and left his office, heading toward the upper levels of the mountain.

It wasn't quite time yet for his official appointment, but that was just too bad. Hammond wanted to talk to the CinC *now*.

As soon as he left his own area, a discreet escort fell into position behind him. He might be supreme in his own bailiwick, but once outside it he was subject to regular CMC security.

Rude, very rude to barge in on the commanding general this way. In medieval times, Hammond would have used a herald with a trumpet to request a rendezvous on neutral ground where two sovereign lords could treat with each other as equals. Pace would have taken his time about considering the request and then responded via a herald of his own.

Hammond had no intention of getting medieval. He charged ahead, letting his escort fall further and further behind, and burst through clusters of frantically saluting military types like a gun dog flushing coveys of quail.

The airman serving as receptionist outside Pace's office shot to his feet and quivered at full attention in the dazzle of Hammond's general's stars.

"At ease," Hammond snapped, returning the salute. "Austin in there?"

"Um, he's in a meeting with Brigadier Cassidy," the airman quavered.

"Hmph. See if he's got a spare scone for me."

The airman swallowed and reached for a telephone, speaking softly and rapidly into it while Hammond let go a long breath and wondered suddenly if this was such a good idea after all. He didn't mind facing down Pace; Cassidy was something else. He was willing to tear into Pace anytime, but he'd never quite understood the mild-mannered, steel-spined Canadian. Cassidy wasn't quite British, but he sometimes behaved like the very image of the upper-crust, not-quite-all-there aristocrat—and he was assuredly both present and accounted for at all times. Hammond sometimes thought that without Cassidy, Pace would be completely lost as commander of Cheyenne Mountain. He didn't bother to wonder what either man thought of him, of course.

He briefly considered going back to his office and

going through channels after all—no, that would look too much like a retreat—when the door opened and Pace appeared, not at all surprised by Hammond's early, if infuriated, arrival. "George, great to see you! Come on in. Ed and I were just having a little chat about things."

"Scone, George?" Cassidy offered hospitably. The Canadian was attired in semi-dress uniform, with epaulets and ribbons galore. The creases in his trousers could cut glass. His black shoes gleamed with a mirror finish. By contrast, though Austin Pace could pass inspection by the most critical U.S. master sergeant, the American general in *his* uniform looked just the least bit disheveled.

Hammond nodded, deciding not to be put off, and took a chair across a low table from the other two men. He could play civilized with the best of them. "Thanks. Skipped breakfast this morning." The scone disappeared quickly and efficiently, taking just enough time for Hammond to observe the twinkle in Cassidy's eye, the deep-seated dissatisfaction in Pace's.

"All right," he said, washing down the last bit and setting his coffee mug down on the table with a decisive click. "Let's get to the point. Austin, what's this I hear about you letting reporters in for a tour?"

"One reporter," Pace corrected automatically. "And that's not what he's coming as."

"Yeah, Army beats Navy every single year," Hammond snorted. "And I've got a pig who makes a great copilot."

Cassidy chuckled openly. Hammond glared. Cassidy chuckled again.

"He's going to be escorted every minute," Pace said. "Yes, we're doing this as a favor to his father, but he's not going anywhere near your bailiwick. And we have a few things *we'd* rather not share, too, you know." He glanced pointedly at the door to his office, outside of which Hammond's escort waited patiently. Need to Know cut both ways. "I don't intend to lose control of the situation, George."

Hammond grunted, not yet sure he was mollified. "You're taking all precautions, of course."

"Naturally," Pace said frostily. "Kinsey will be under escort at all times. We're not interested in turning loose a reporter any more than you are. Particularly this one. He's got a reputation as a good reporter, been in action. I've talked to some of my colleagues, and they say he's had the opportunity to blow operations and knew when to keep his mouth shut. But he's also fried a couple of commanders for breakfast for stupid decisions, cost them their careers. You heard about the Pinxley scandal? That was Kinsey."

Cassidy added, "We're told he's doing a review piece for the *Washington Observer* on the current state of space defense. I think we've got more to worry about than you do, George."

Hammond doubted that—the existence of NORAD, at least, wasn't any secret—but he decided to borrow a tactic from Sun Tzu and change directions, at least for the moment. Kinsey might have precipitated his coming up here ahead of schedule, but they did still have an agenda for this meeting, and he wanted to get those issues sorted out too. "All right. I'll take your word for it for the time being—let's not borrow trouble. As long as I'm here, let's get to business. We've got some other problems to talk about—they're on the memo I sent up earlier."

"Oh, *challenges*, surely, George? Let's not characterize them as problems before we've even had a chance to look at them." Cassidy set his cup back on the saucer with a discreet clatter of porcelain. The Canadian supplied his own cup; both Pace and Hammond preferred mugs for their caffeine, the larger the better.

"Well, I must say it certainly was a *challenge* to find out how you proposed to refit your entire internal

communications system at Blue Book's expense."
Hammond settled back into his leather chair to begin
battle. He could feel his initial anger at the identity
of the reporter ebbing as they moved on to more
mundane issues. It wasn't NORAD's fault, after all.
And maybe it would turn out to be only a tempest
in a teapot after all.

Pace coughed as a swallow of scone went down
the wrong way. Cassidy smiled peacefully, maintaining a position as neutral observer, rather like a
judge at a tennis match. Point to Hammond for the
unexpected serve.

"You admitted that it was your project that practically brought the mountain down around our ears,"
Pace volleyed back once the obstruction in his throat
had been cleared. "And our memorandum of understanding when you moved in clearly stated that you
would assume all costs of . . ."

"And we have. We fixed our little problem. Haven't
had any vibration for, oh, months. Have we?"

"The damage still exists. And you have an obligation
to assist us in maintaining our battle readiness—"

"*Which* I have done, and continue to do. Those
repairs were made, Austin, and you know it. What
you're asking for now amounts to a complete upgrade of internal communications for the whole
damn mountain, and that's unreasonable."

"I see no reason why—"

"I do. We're very much aware that you've been a
gracious host, and we've tried to be a cooperative
guest, but the fact that we've had a shakedown
cruise"—he ignored Cassidy's snort of amusement at
the pun—"in no way implies that you can use us to
justify your brand-new bells and whistles."

Pace glared. "George, are you *sure* you're not a
Navy man?"

"No, but I can swear like a sailor if you want me
to."

"All right, all right." Pace lifted a hand in defeat. "I'll have my financial people look at the numbers again. It's possible they could have misplaced a decimal point."

Hammond just barely refrained from expressing raw skepticism. It was rather more than *one* decimal point. He'd won, though, and he knew better than to gloat. Next time it would be Pace's turn, and Hammond would be the one having to back down on an issue. Best not to leave ill feelings behind.

"All right, then. We may be able to contribute something to the communications interface. I'll see if I've got anything left in the budget that will help." He was feeling downright generous now, and decided to close one more loop on the original subject while he was at it. "Oh yes, one more thing about our unexpected visitor. I'd like a full itinerary sent down to my Chief of Staff's office, if you don't mind, so I'll know where to keep my people away from. And some information about his escort, too."

"Well, that part shouldn't present any problems." Pace was visibly relieved at the relaxing of tension in the room. "The escort has already been fully briefed and knows the ropes. He's one of yours, in fact."

"Oh?" One brow arched high. "How do you mean, one of mine?"

"Yes," Pace went on, warming to the concept. He actually leaned forward across his desk, clasping his hands together. "The escort used to work for you right here in the Complex, in fact. It's Bert Samuels. Lieutenant Colonel Bert Samuels."

"Major Morley." Janet Frasier's soft voice demanded Morley's attention as he sat numbly at the table. The rest of the meeting had long since packed itself up and headed to its respective next stops. Even Frasier had left. He was the only one with no place to go. He had no idea how long he'd been sitting, but it didn't matter, did it?

And now the doctor was back. He closed his eyes. He didn't want to deal with the chief medical officer again.

"Major." She wasn't going to go away.

"What do you want?" He didn't bother to open his eyes to look at her. It was nice and dark and safe behind his eyelids, and he didn't have to see the looks on the faces of the others, the contempt, the disgust, the pity. He saw enough other things behind his closed eyelids to punish himself with; he didn't need the so-called empathy of his so-called peers on top of it.

"I'd like you to come back to Medical with me," she said.

He could hear the rustle of her crisp slacks as she slid into the chair next to him. One cool hand covered his intertwined fingers—without pressure, without anything other than simple human contact. Behind his eyelids, he could feel the burning of salt.

"I know that you're profoundly upset," she went on. "I'd like to prescribe something to help you through the next couple of days. Nothing long-term."

He inhaled sharply, the force of it lifting his head up and back, and then let it go and got up, pulling his hands out from under hers as he shoved back his chair and moved around the table to stand by the window wall that overlooked Level C-2. Almost two stories below, he could see figures moving around the Stargate and its metal ramp, like ants cleaning up around their nest or scavenging for food. A series of probes were lined up like patient donkeys, waiting their turn to be used. Technicians were still giving them last-minute checks.

The Gate belched open abruptly, and he flinched at the roar and billow of blue plasma. By the time the roiling energy had settled into the shimmering surface that was the entrance to the wormhole between worlds, he had recovered himself. He was peripherally aware of Frasier standing beside him, watching as the first probe rolled forward, into the shimmer, and vanished.

"Amazing, isn't it," she said. She was watching the activity below them, as technicians began recording data about the probe's journey through the warp of space and about its nearly instantaneous arrival at its destination, lit by a sun unimaginably far away. Several of the technicians were gathered now around the main data console, pointing out details to each other from the various displays. The probes gathered information ranging from atmospheric and meteorological to visual scans of its immediate vicinity and transmitted them back to Earth—the only kind of transmission that could be sent through the wormhole in reverse.

"Yeah," he answered at last. "Amazing. It sure is." Nothing in his tone reflected the sense of his words. "People ought to know about it."

"I used to dream about going into space," she remarked wistfully. "Rocket ships and *Stand By For Mars!* Did you read science fiction when you were a kid, Major?"

He shook his head abruptly, as if casting off some minor irritation. "Still do. Brin, Clement, Pournelle. But it's nothing like what's out there." He turned away from the window as the Gate closed. The sudden cessation of noise rang in their ears.

The technicians below would try to contact the probe again later, assuming the doughty little machine survived. Meanwhile, there were others waiting to go as soon as new coordinates and new worlds could be located. "What's out there is just like here. Just as bad. War is war no matter where it is."

Frasier's brows arched in surprise. "Surely not? They're alien worlds, after all."

"They're war zones," he snapped. "The weapons are a little different, maybe, but that's all. Maybe the things using them aren't . . ." He stopped abruptly.

She tilted her head, thinking about it. "I don't agree. The teams have told us about too many different worlds, different people. They're not all humans, seeded by the Goa'uld. There are adventures out there."

For the first time he looked her full in the face, the overhead light catching the bruises on his face and making them stand out with brutal clarity. "There's death out there, Doctor. Death and a war we can't win. We ought to shut the damn Gate down and forget about poking sticks at the System Lords and everything else out there. One of these days we're going to poke too hard. They're going to come after us sooner or later, and when they do they're going to win. We might as well just get ready for it."

"Rather defeatist, don't you think?" she said mildly.

"Realistic," he snapped. "And forget about drugging me up, Doctor. I don't need any chemical help to know what day it is. We ought to be protecting our own turf, building up our own defenses. People ought to know what's going on. Because one of these days the Jaffa are going to arrive and catch this whole world flat-footed, and people are going to die just like my team died."

It was always easier to admit being defeated by an invincible enemy, she thought. If failure was inevitable, there wasn't any shame in failing.

"I know there are people who agree with you, Major. Politicians—"

"Like Kinsey. He had the right idea. Shut the damn thing down."

"Nonetheless," she said firmly, "I expect you in my office in the next twenty minutes, Major. I understand that this mission was a terrible blow, but you haven't had time to build any kind of perspective about it. All I want to do is give you a head start on objectivity."

"Objectivity," he repeated, with a hollow chuckle. "How many casualties does it take to be objective?"

"Twenty minutes, Major." She made a point of checking the time on her wristwatch, glanced once more at him, and then made her way out of the room.

Morley's behavior, while more extreme than some, was certainly understandable, she thought. He was a good man, a poor leader, and had severely bad luck. None of that was his fault.

She hoped he really would show up down in Medical; she had an antidepressant in mind that would do wonders for him for the time being. Meanwhile, she'd look in on the casualties and make sure there weren't any changes on that front.

He'd set foot on an alien world, felt the light of an alien star, and didn't even appreciate it. Life, she concluded, wasn't fair.

Normally George Hammond was cool, calm, and self-possessed. He prided himself on his ability to remain calm under fire.

There were some things, however, that would make him go up like a Titan rocket, and that name was one of them.

"*Who?*" he roared, launching himself out of his chair and slamming his palms down on Pace's maple guest table. The tea tray bounced and clattered. He wasn't so far gone that he couldn't hear, behind him, the sudden stillness coming from Cassidy; it was enough to let him catch hold of himself before the second stage of his temper ignited.

"Samuels. Bert Samuels. Used to be your aide, assigned here, if I'm not mistaken." Pace wasn't about to be pushed around. "Sit down, dammit, George, you're going to give yourself a heart attack. What's the big deal about Samuels, anyway?"

"That little—" Hammond caught himself abruptly. It would be poor politics—poor *tactics*—to admit that Samuels, who, after all, had more intimate knowledge of Project Blue Book—as the Stargate project was now known outside its own confines—than either of the other two men in the room, was a conniving little—

He sat back down and composed himself.

"Let's just say that Samuels isn't the person I would have chosen for the job," he said icily. "But it doesn't surprise me in the least. He's been associated with the senator. It makes sense that he'd volunteer to escort the son. You're going to find yourselves on the front page of the *Washington Observer*, you know."

"While you and Blue Book hide discreetly behind our skirts."

Hammond looked Pace in the eye. "You're damned right."

Pace sat back in his chair and said nothing.

Hammond took a deep breath. "All right. I don't want him anywhere near my project, but we all understand that. I don't like Samuels escorting him, but that's out of our hands. How long is he supposed to be here?"

"Three hours," Cassidy responded. The Canadian brigadier had taken the opportunity, while Hammond and Pace spoke, to review the schedule for the day. "The regular briefing in the Visitors Center, a few minutes to clear the area, and then Samuels will bring him inside. We'll meet with him and give him the old God-Save-the-Queen, er, Republic, speeches. He should be in our actual hair for only an hour or so, from about 1300 to 1400, and shouldn't have anything to do with you lot at all."

Hammond nodded sharply in approval. "All right

then. We'll take the appropriate actions." He was still seething; every time that name came up—either name in fact, Kinsey *or* Samuels—it meant trouble. He should never have lost it that way. Cassidy and Pace were exchanging meaningful glances over his head as it was.

He took a deep breath and tried to bring the discussion back to the regular Friday agenda. "All right, you can tell that Samuels isn't my favorite person, but I'm going to trust you to keep him and his tame reporter where they belong. Meanwhile, let's deal with some of the other issues on the table and see if we can get back to business. My personnel tell me they're getting some flak from your procurement people—"

The meeting turned to more everyday matters of how to keep a large facility with thousands of employees and billions of dollars' worth of equipment running smoothly and in a state of constant readiness. Systems and procedures were reviewed. Decisions were made. Scones were consumed. By the time they were finished, all three men were well satisfied that operations would continue uninterrupted for at least another week, without undue friction between the ostensible mission of the Complex and the black op that functioned in its shadow.

It was eleven-thirty when George Hammond left the CinC's office, heading back to his own demesne. Time, he thought, for lunch, to be followed by the latest information review and preparation for his weekly update to the President. Which would definitely include a few comments about some interfering Senators and their sons.

Just another damned day at the office.

CHAPTER SIX

Frank Kinsey sat across a restaurant table from Lieutenant Colonel Bert Samuels and contemplated the massive hamburger and mountain of steak fries on the colonel's plate. The cholesterol from the mayonnaise alone should be enough to hospitalize the man.

And maybe that would be a good thing. He was beginning to be actively annoyed at the self-satisfied smirk that had taken up permanent residence on the man's face. He was very tired of the "I-know-something-you-don't know" attitude.

The restaurant was one of those down-home places with farm implements on the wall and red-checked tablecloths, just off the state highway leading south out of Colorado Springs. It specialized in "American food," like hamburgers and fried chicken and meat loaf. Most of its clientele seemed to consist of service personnel from the nearby base and truckers handling semis across the Colorado Rockies. The food in the place actually smelled pretty good, if you liked grease.

"I don't know how you can eat that stuff," Samuels said, dolloping a large glop of catsup over his fries.

Kinsey smiled vaguely and dug into the big scoop of tuna on top of three kinds of lettuce, discreetly edging the slice of hard-boiled egg off to one side. He'd been surprised to find a whole section of "healthy alternatives" on the menu. Grease *and* tuna. Go figure.

"What are you, some kind of vegetarian?" Samuels said the word as if he wouldn't be surprised in the least that the man across from him was such a reactionary.

Kinsey forked in a mouthful of fish and smiled. "Watching my weight."

Samuels snorted and picked up a knife and fork and started cutting up the hamburger. Kinsey paused in mid-chew in surprise.

"Little trick I picked up in London," Samuels said. "Nobody eats with their hands over there. It's considered very rude."

Kinsey, who had spent some time on the British beat himself, nodded. He *had* seen the British eating that way. It struck him as a bit pretentious to do such a thing in Colorado Springs, Colorado. Maybe Samuels was trying to impress him with how cosmopolitan he was. But then, Kinsey had also seen the Brits eating vinegar-soaked fish and chips out of a newspaper cone, so maybe Samuels wasn't as cosmopolitan as he thought he was.

"You're going to see some amazing things this afternoon," Samuels promised, reaching for a soaked french fry—with his fingers, Kinsey noticed. So much for "British" decorum. "The things that go on in that mountain are just beyond belief."

"North American Aerospace Defense? I still don't see what's new about that." Kinsey pretended not to be interested. The *Observer* editor really did want a story; access to the actual interior of the complex had been shut down some time ago, all allegedly "for security reasons." He supposed that was why he'd gotten saddled with Samuels, his father's military liaison guy. It didn't mean he had to like it. In his experience, military escorts meant making sure he didn't see anything good. When he said so, the senator and the colonel had exchanged one of those I-know-something glances, as if they had a huge surprise waiting for him. "Let me guess. They brought one of the Roswell aliens to Cheyenne Mountain and they're interrogating it even as we speak."

Samuels coughed, spraying a fine mist of red condiment across the table. Kinsey could see red flecks across the beige tuna where there hadn't been any red flecks before, and he pushed his salad away, deciding he wasn't all that hungry any more anyway. There weren't any public dining facilities at CMAS, but he figured he could last until dinnertime. As long as he didn't have to share dinner with this guy.

"Oh, no," Samuels said as soon as he cleared his throat. "No, no no. Roswell. Ha ha. That's funny. That was a weather balloon."

The waitress came by and Kinsey shifted his plate at her, silently asking her to take it away.

"Something wrong?" she asked.

"No, nothing's wrong. I'm just not hungry. I'll have another cup of coffee, thanks."

Samuels was deep into another bite of hamburger, trying to hold the bun and meat on an upside-down fork with his knife. He might have picked up the trick in England, Kinsey thought, but he certainly hadn't practiced it much.

"You'll get the regular briefing along with everybody else at the Visitors Center," Samuels mumbled. "Then you'll get to go inside. No cameras or tape recorders, of course. But you'll see . . ." He swallowed, reached for a napkin to pat his lips. "You'll see some really interesting things at Cheyenne Mountain Air Station. USSPACECOM is in there too. You'll get to see the satellite tracking, Air Defense Ops, Satellite Warning, Combined Intelligence—"

"Space Control," Kinsey interrupted in a bored voice. "I *know* all this stuff already. I know it's important and 'essential to the national security.' I just don't see that it's *interesting*. The Cold War is over. Unless you think the Chinese or the Serbs are going to launch missiles at us, who cares?"

The waitress brought his coffee, complete with a couple of miniature cream containers. He pried one open, only to find that it had gone beyond clotted and well into sour.

Black coffee. Wonderful. And it wasn't decaf, either. Just what he needed at an altitude of more than a mile—he was going to have a case of the raving jitters before this day was through.

Samuels made a point of waiting until the waitress was out of earshot. "I don't think you give us enough credit," he said mysteriously. "More things in heaven and earth, you know. That's Shakespeare."

Kinsey sighed and shook his head. Dad—or maybe Mom, he couldn't decide—owed him one for this, he thought. Even if he didn't have any more interesting assignments on tap, he could have spent this time fishing or something. But no, he was going to be dragged into an Air Force public relations tour. He'd get paid for it. Big hairy deal.

The check came, and the two men paid their bill and made their way out into the bright mountain sunshine. Nice little town, Colorado Springs, Kinsey thought. Pretty. Peaceful. Home to the Air Force Academy, the Canadian Forces Support Unit (Colorado Springs), the hundreds or thousands of military personnel and all their dependents who served at Peterson and Falcon Air Force Bases and Fort Carson, and, of course, to Cheyenne Mountain Air Station. Pretty big responsibility for a pretty little town.

Well, maybe not that little. The metropolitan area, spread out under the benign, ever-snowcapped guardianship of Pikes Peak, was nearly half a million strong. There had to be *something* besides the military and unsolved murders keeping Colorado Springs thriving.

They got into the rental car and started the drive up to the mountain, leaving the pretty, peaceful little company city behind.

Teal'C had never been to Roswell, though O'Neill thought he might take the Jaffa there sometime, just for the hell of it. Then he could claim there really *had* been an alien in the little New Mexico town, at least once. It was the kind of in-joke that appealed to him. Maybe he'd suggest it to the whole team, though Carter would argue about it. Carter always argued. It was one of the delightful aspects of her personality.

He was getting a case of pre-mission nerves again, he could tell. It had been too long since SG-1 had actually been through the Gate—at least two weeks. He wanted to get out and *do* something. Scrabbling in his desk, he found a cache of rubber bands and began firing them at the poster on the opposite wall.

Carter and Jackson might view the down time as a great opportunity to extend their studies in astrophysics and anthropology, respectively, but O'Neill was sure that Teal'C, at least, shared his need to be active, to actually accomplish something. Every day that went by was one more day his people, his family were held in slavery by the Goa'uld.

Stacked on his desk were volumes of reports, the printed version of several CDs' worth of accumulated information on the Goa'uld, the Nox, the crystals of P3X-562, and all the other worlds, races, and entities they'd met so far. SG-1 was responsible for most of that information. O'Neill wanted to go get more information, and let the desk pilots like Randolph and Rusalka scrabble through it day in and day out.

From his point of view, the most fruitful mission would be one to the location he had mentally dubbed the "war world." It held the possibility of finding new allies and new weapons they could use against the Goa'uld. The Goa'uld might be one side of the war, in fact, and if that was the case he wouldn't mind joining in a firefight or two. Strictly in the course of achieving his mission's primary goal, naturally.

Squinting, he incorporated a worn-down pencil into his artillery. It bounced harmlessly off Antares. He huffed out an exasperated breath. He wanted to *move*, dammit, and trying to push Rusalka into making a recommendation before she was ready was an exercise in futility.

Maybe he could pick up something from Morley. He'd buy the poor guy a drink in the canteen, pump him about the tactics the Jaffa had used to lure him in. He had a feeling that Morley knew more than he was telling—the report was curiously flat, without much substance to it. It was a little mystery, what had gone so thoroughly wrong on Etaa. Maybe Teal'C could get something out of the major—no, bringing the Jaffa along, with his forehead brand marking him as the property of Apophis, was probably a bad idea. Morley wouldn't want to deal with him. In fact, it was his attitude toward the other man that had led to O'Neill's negative recommendation in the first place.

Although, dammit, Teal'C was on their side, and he might have some valuable insights. Morley was going to *have* to learn to deal with the Jaffa eventually. Hammond had wanted to give Morley a chance, despite O'Neill's views on the subject, and had allowed him to command SG-2 for the Etaa recovery. And look where *that* led.

Spilled milk buttered no parsnips. O'Neill bounced to his feet. This time of day Teal'C was probably in either the armory or the gym. He'd go find him and then they'd hunt down Morley, find out whatever it was he was holding back about Etaa. Maybe he could change the general's mind about going back, and he could find out what really happened to the tall, gentle people who lived there.

It was a plan. More important, it was something to *do*.

The first stop, of course, was the research office again. Randolph didn't even look up as he came in, and Rusalka gave him an annoyed glare and shake of the head when he demanded, "Either of you know where Dave Morley is?"

Outside the office, Dave Morley, on his way to Medical, heard his name mentioned and paused to eavesdrop, trying to hear what the infamous O'Neill had to say about him.

Shamelessly, the infamous O'Neill looked over Randolph's shoulder at the pile of paper her printer was spitting out in a steady stream. "What's this all about?"

He picked up the pile of paper and began shuffling through it. "Articles? *Post*. *NewsWorld*. *LA Times*. 'Secrets and the Public's Right to Know.' Op-ed? They're all by Frank Kinsey. That's interesting . . ."

"That's for General Hammond," Randolph growled, still bending over a hot keyboard as she searched for more articles through an international library database.

"And why is General Hammond so interested in Frank Kinsey, modern journalist?" he wanted to know. "And what relation is he to our not-so-loved Senator Kinsey?"

"His son, and he's coming out to the complex today. *Not* to visit us," Rusalka forestalled the colonel's reaction with a hastily raised hand. "Apparently just being a tourist."

"Apparently just jerking our chain, more like it." O'Neill growled. "Is he coming here?"

"Not supposed to," Rusalka reiterated patiently. "If you don't mind, Colonel, we're putting together a background briefing, just in case. And no," she added as he opened his mouth, "I haven't the faintest idea where Major Morley is. It wasn't my turn to watch him."

Outside the office, Major Morley stood indecisively for a moment, and then turned away—away from the conversation in the staff office, which wasn't about him after all, and away from Medical and his appointment with Janet Frasier.

A sudden emergency claimed Dr. Frasier's attention. One of the survivors of the incident on Etaa went into full cardiac arrest, and it took all the skills she and Dr. Warner and a full complement of surgical staff could muster to get the man's heart back into a steady rhythm. Then they had to determine how they'd missed the problem to begin with. The man was one of several who had injuries not consistent with Jaffa weaponry. She'd told Hammond— she'd told the airman—that they were all going to live, and they would if she had anything to say about it. So it was considerably more than twenty minutes later when she glanced up at the wall clock and realized that David Morley had never reported in as ordered.

She considered having him paged and decided against it. The man was under stress as it was, and he obviously felt that he had screwed up, that everyone in the complex was accusing him.

Time, perhaps, for her to take a break anyway and go looking for him. She peeled off the last set of gloves and untied her surgical mask, and then paused. She could at least ask Security if he'd left the complex, and if not, she could go enlist Sam to help her. He'd probably consider two women less threatening than one determined doctor by herself, and maybe they could just talk to him over lunch. Or listen to him over lunch. Whatever it took to get him to come down to Medical and get meds.

Samantha Carter was neck-deep in fifth-order mathematics and utterly happy. One of her duties, or perhaps her obsessions, was trying to figure out how the Stargate actually worked—what triggered the opening of the wormhole, why waves and photons could go both ways through it but nothing else could, the back-calculation of where worlds had been when the table of coordinates had been made up and where those worlds were now. She was hunched over her desk, a towel slung around her neck, dressed in T-shirt and fatigues, sharing the lab with half a dozen other scientists who were working on much the same problems. Most of them, of course, were in uniform, but the few civilians working on the project didn't have a dress code and wouldn't know what to do with it if they did. It made for a relaxed atmosphere. Carter wasn't reporting anywhere today that she knew of, so she figured she might as well just be comfortable.

At one end of the lab was an electronic whiteboard covered in symbols at least as cryptic as the Goa'uld glyphs. A couple of civilians dressed in jeans and Birkenstocks were arguing in soft voices in front of the board, in an ongoing discussion about whether one particular sign should be positive, negative, or perhaps some third fuzzy state dependent on an earlier section of the equation. Carter was just as well pleased that her current problem dealt with an entirely different aspect of the wormhole. She was working on a method of predicting the next Gate location. If it worked, she hoped to be able eventually to extrapolate backward and perhaps, one day, find the homeworld of the aliens who had originally built the system of Gates.

Every once in a while a piece of the puzzle seemed to fall into place, leading one inch closer to solution. A private puzzle with a public solution, one day. Or at least so she hoped.

"Hey, Sam."

She looked up to find Dr. Frasier looking around the doorjamb. "Yo?"

"Have you seen Major Morley?"

Carter blinked. "Uh. No." She looked up at the clock on the wall, was startled to find that it was long after noon already. No wonder her stomach was rumbling.

Frasier looked concerned. Carter closed her laptop screen and got up, leaving the discussion and the lovely, ordered world of mathematics behind, and joined the doctor.

"He was supposed to report to me in Medical," Frasier explained. "That was over an hour ago. I'm a bit worried about him."

"He didn't seem very happy this morning," Sam agreed. "I only saw him briefly, though."

"At least he hasn't left the complex. Maybe he's in his quarters."

"Have you asked Security to find him for you?"

"I don't want to make a fuss about it. I'm trying to convince him this is not that big a deal. I'm getting worried, though."

"I'll help you look."

Having discovered Teal'C in the gymnasium as expected, O'Neill explained what he wanted to the Jaffa as they swept down the corridors to the last likely place an anguished officer might hide out. Teal'C was more interested in the gossip about the senator's son than he was about interrogating Morley; his impression of the former commander of SG-2 was extremely low. Nonetheless, O'Neill was right; it was something to do. So the massive Jaffa went along. He could always return to the weight machines later.

The "Officers' Club" buried in the heart of the mountain was pretty much like every other such club on every other military base: a bar, some small tables, and a few larger tables for civilized meals. The only difference was that this club was considerably smaller than the average, and thus, there was no regular Saturday bingo.

The place wasn't even official. The *real* Officers' Club was at Peterson in Colorado Springs.

Still, there had to be someplace a man could get a beer without driving all the way down the mountain and back again. Thus, the Club. Paralleled, of course, by the NCO and EM clubs, which among them divided up the triangular bar. The Blue Book Recreation Services budget had limits, after all.

Teal'C followed O'Neill into the Officers' Club like a large silent shadow. A few men sitting at one of the round tables, noshing down on chicken sandwiches and chips and the occasional lite beer, waved acknowledgment to the two of them. O'Neill waved back; Teal'C nodded briefly. The two of them scanned the rest of the place, and O'Neill's eyes lit up at the sight of the other occupant of the place.

Morley was seated at the bar, glumly picking at a bowl of peanuts. He flinched when Teal'C appeared beside him, only to find O'Neill sliding onto the stool on the other side. The major looked at the two of them and closed his eyes in misery.

"So, Dave," O'Neill began, not bothering with preliminaries. "Tough mission. But you know, I was thinking, we need a little bit more information. These Jaffa you ran into, and that force field you say they had—"

Morley spun around on his barstool, nearly knocking the colonel down. "You weren't there!"

O'Neill paused, then carefully moved the glass bowl of peanuts to the middle of the polished surface of the bar, his sharp brown eyes never leaving Morley's. The glass made a scraping sound against the wood. "No," he said quietly. He dropped all vestiges of casual hail-fellow-well-met, and his voice became serious, his manner intent. "I wasn't there. Not this time, at least.

"So tell me about it. You had no reason to expect trouble. You didn't see anything? No hints at all?" His tone was conversational. On the other side, Teal'C somehow managed to give the man more room without perceptibly moving.

"They pulled us in. They flanked us. How was I supposed to know they were there?"

"The Jaffa have set traps before." Teal'C's voice was a rumble.

O'Neill barely flicked a glance at his teammate, and the Jaffa subsided. "That's the thing about traps," he agreed. "You don't know they're there."

"We saw the stuff originally reported," Morley went on. "The buildings. The towers. But no sign of Jaffa. Not even in the, the, the compound where they *rounded everybody up*. We thought we could—"

"They're beginning to expect us," O'Neill interrupted Morley's rising, increasingly agitated rant. "We're moving to a new level now. They figure when we come through we'll come through again. They're setting traps for us."

He shifted his gaze to Teal'C. "Do you think this is a general plan? Or do we have one bright Jaffa on P7X-924? Whaddaya think, Teal'C?"

Teal'C frowned even more deeply than usual. "It is possible that this is an innovation by a single squad leader," he said. "We have not seen this response before. Usually, a compound is emptied quickly and the Jaffa leave."

"They *trapped* us," Morley said. "They know how to beat us. Every time we go through the Gate they're going to kill us." He gripped his glass hard, his fingers white and red against the glass. "We've got to stop. We have to shut it down."

"No can do, Major," O'Neill said, still using the calm, uninflected tone with which he might address a frightened animal or an irrational officer. "We've got orders."

"Fuck orders!"

"Now that wouldn't be any fun at all," O'Neill said evenly. "Besides, Morley, we've got people back there. And we don't leave people behind."

The officers across the room were watching them openly now, attracted by Morley's raised voice.

"You don't understand," he said, even louder. "They were *my* people. The ones we went in there to save, they were all gone already. So it's my people—they were my— Not yours! And they're dead. They're all dead by now. And you know we can't win. We can't possibly win." *Rivers of tar. Beating of wings. The Jaffa screamed too, like human beings.* "People need to know. They're going to come and kill us all—"

"That's defeatism, son," O'Neill said mildly. "And besides, I don't believe it." The glass bowl rotated against the bar, scraping gently against the wood. Morley jerked at the sound, and O'Neill's long fingers paused in response.

"I don't care what you believe!" the major snapped. "I'm telling you the truth. We've got no choice." He made as if to get up. The colonel rose more quickly, forestalling him.

"Major"—there was a razor edge to O'Neill's voice now—"you'd better care. I'm putting you under house arrest. Report to your quarters until further notice."

"You can't—"

O'Neill smiled without humor and lifted one hand to tap the silver eagle perched on his right shoulder. "Yes, I can. Colonel, see?" He pointed at the gold oak leaves that adorned Morley's. "Major."

Morley stared at him, licked his lips, and glanced at Teal'C. "You. You're one of them. You're part of it."

"That will be *enough*, Major!" O'Neill's voice was a whiplash. The officers across the room decided that elsewhere was a very good place to be.

"Well, that's settled," O'Neill said as the two men walked out of the club.

"What is settled?"

"Where we're going next. We're going to finish the job." O'Neill's tone was still quiet and conversational. Teal'C thought he detected a layer of seething rage beneath it.

"You do not believe, then, that the members of SG-2 left behind are all dead." The two men walked shoulder to shoulder down the hall, taking up most of the space between the walls.

"I believe that Dave Morley isn't giving us the whole story, and if there's more to Jaffa tactics, we'd better know about it."

"Do you think General Hammond will approve such a mission for SG-1?"

"I think he might, yeah."

And if he didn't? Teal'C wondered. He decided to prepare himself for travel anyway, just in case.

CHAPTER SEVEN

Dad thought that shock of white hair reminded his constituents of Edward Everett Dirksen. He didn't care whether they'd liked Dirksen or not; the name and the white hair were famous, and had clout, and that was all he cared about.

They were in the study of the Georgetown place, sharing brandy and cigars after a good meal. Mother had rolled her eyes and gone elsewhere when Dad had suggested "a little postprandial treat."

It wasn't a bad cigar. Not Cuban, but not bad. Frank leaned back in his leather chair and looked up through the cloud of aromatic smoke to the shelves of books behind his father. At least they weren't all the same color and size— Mother probably had something to do with that—but he was willing to bet that his father the senator hadn't opened one since his parents had moved in three terms ago. Strictly for show, strictly to impress the voters. He'd become resigned to knowing that about his father long ago.

"So, boy, I read your little piece in the Post," his father grinned, swirling dark amber liquid around in the globe glass. "Taking your old dad to task again, are you?"

He smiled to disguise his sigh. It was always like this. He kept coming to dinner to please Mother, and every time, Dad tried to bait him about something.

"It wasn't directed specifically at you," he pointed out. "I just think this whole isolationist trend is damaging in the long run."

"Humph." Senator Kinsey sipped, holding the liquor in his mouth, savoring it. "Keeps our boys from getting killed."

"While a lot of other people die."

"They don't pay taxes here."

And they don't vote, Frank added mentally.

"Well, be that as it may." A billow of smoke issued from the old man's mouth, on either side of the cigar he held between his teeth. "There are some things you just don't want following you home, boy. There are limits."

"Refusing to open our borders to people in need—"

"We've got enough problems right here! Those folks will come in and take our jobs, use our resources—"

"Like Grandpa did when he came over from England?"

A moment later he was sorry he'd snapped at the old man. The senator was staring at him almost malevolently. He'd have to apologize to Mother before he left. Again. The leather of his chair squeaked as he shifted his weight to place the snifter on an end table.

"What would it take to convince you, boy?"

"Convince me of what, sir?" He still called his father sir, even when he was on the verge of walking out on him. Old habits were hard to break.

"That some doors need to be shut—" The old man's jaws clamped hard on the cigar, as if a thought had just occurred to him. "Well," he resumed after a moment, "I don't suppose it's worth fighting about. You had a pretty rough time on that last assignment, didn't you?"

"Tough enough." Frank sat back warily. This was the first time his father had voluntarily given up a fight, beaten or not, and they hadn't even reached the shouting stage yet.

"Got anything else lined up just now?"

He shook his head. "I'm thinking of just taking it easy for a while."

Senator Kinsey chortled. "Another one of your unpaid vacations, eh? Well, I had an idea."

Alarm bells rang in the back of the journalist's head.
"What kind of idea?"

"Now don't get your back hair up, boy. I was just talking the other day to the editor of the Washington Observer, and he mentioned he wanted some kind of article about NORAD. You know about NORAD, don't you?"

"Yeah. I've heard of it." *He tried hard to keep the suspicion out of his voice.*

"Well, it's based out there in Colorado, in the mountains. Good air. Relaxing place. I said I thought I might be able to talk you into doing a little something for him on your break. I know some of those folks out there, y'know." *The Senator grinned complacently and set the stub of his cigar aside in an ashtray. A thin line of smoke continued to rise from it, as if from a tube of incense.* "Seems that Dale Terwilliger, that's the editor, he was downright impressed that a 'writer of your stature'— that's what he called it, 'stature.' When did you get yourself stature, boy?—might be willing to do a few words for him on Space Defense."

The Observer paid a decent word rate, as he recalled. It also reached an audience that was more aligned with his own philosophy than his father's. He wondered just how his father had come to have this conversation with Terwilliger.

"How does he want it slanted?" *he asked cynically.*

"Why, he didn't say a thing about that. I think he just wants your view of the place. Your mother thinks it's a fine idea—I can even get you inside. Hardly anybody gets inside that mountain anymore, you know."

His father knew all his buttons. But still—maybe it would be interesting. He doubted it, but a paid vacation was always better than an unpaid one. "I'll call him and see what he wants. I'm not in the business of doing party propaganda for you, Dad."

"Wouldn't dream of asking you to, boy. I just think, well, now, my boy's a good investigative reporter. Every-

body says so. So why not have him look at NORAD? It's a nice change of pace. Besides, you never know what you might find there."

"Most of that stuff's classified."

"I thought you believed in the people's right to know."

Or maybe it was the people's right to be bored. Terwilliger was enthusiastic about a study of NORAD. Dad had made arrangements. So here he was, still feeling thoroughly manipulated and not at all sure why. Of course, his mother had been delighted that he'd finally allowed his father to "help" him. The fact that he'd probably have been able to swing this article all by himself never occurred to her. Or if it did, she didn't let that bother her.

Frank Kinsey sat back in the contoured chair and looked openly around at the room and its other occupants. The Visitors Center of the Cheyenne Mountain Complex was a small building outside the barbed wire fence, with a circular driveway in front of a polished white portico. The front lobby was filled with models and pictures, and opposite the entrance were two doors leading into the small amphitheatre that served as the Main Briefing room. The chairs for the audience were arranged in descending tiers, facing a small stage with a podium. They were, Kinsey had to admit, remarkably comfortable and well padded, not obviously brand-new but definitely not shabby either. The walls were half-paneled in oak, while the photographs, mounted above the paneling on dry board, were vivid splashes of color, dark and mysterious. The podium was off to one side, allowing plenty of space and a good line of sight to the screen behind it.

The amphitheater, done in colors of blue and gray with soft cream-white walls, could hold perhaps fifty people. Today it was perhaps two-thirds full. It was nicer, he thought, than similar briefing rooms in the Pentagon, but then those weren't generally available to the public. It was miles better than the tents and hotel rooms in the Federal Republic of Yugoslavia, but not quite as nice as the press room in the White House. Here, though, there were no scraps of paper on the floor or burned-out cigarette butts. The place was obsessively clean, as if a master sergeant had made the place his life's work.

He amused himself by speculating about the reasons some of his fellows might have for visiting this rather esoteric tourist spot.

All right, even if he'd been able to swing the article by himself, the senatorial intercession didn't hurt. He didn't like asking his father to use his clout that way, but then, he rationalized, he hadn't asked.

Even the military escort helped a little, he had to admit. It got him in the door, and he was used to working around restrictions. After all, this wasn't the sort of place one came to on the spur of the moment. It took at least two months' advance notice to arrange one of these dog-and-pony shows. So that group of grade-school boys in Cub Scout uniforms, being herded about by a frazzled adult doing a good imitation of a stressed-out Border collie, was most likely here as a field trip. That was no challenge at all.

The couple billing and cooing in the corner had no earthly reason to be here that he could see. They were obviously on a honeymoon, and Frank could think of lots more interesting places to be than here. So . . . maybe they were really spies in deep cover? Russia still had an intelligence service. They could be Chinese recruits. Hmmm. Possible. He wondered how they'd been recruited. They'd have secret meetings with faceless controls. That passion must hide a desperate fear of being discovered.

Sometimes he thought he really ought to try his hand at fiction.

The coterie of middle-aged to elderly men sitting in the front row, all leaning forward with their hands on their knees, had to be either UFO buffs or retired military. Maybe both. The room was cool—air-conditioning hadn't yet been changed over to heat—and the men were still wearing their coats, as if ready to mobilize at a moment's notice. If he listened hard, he could hear the *click-click-click* of loose dentures tapping.

The balance seemed to be just basically curious folks, although the three middle-aged women walking up and down the levels, looking at the pictures on the walls and occasionally whispering to each other and taking notes as they pointed to one detail or another, had to be writers doing research. They had that Look about them.

The pictures were standard public relations scenes. The entrance to the Complex—the fence topped with rolls of razor-sharp barbed wire, the dozen or so tall light poles, the roof of the guard station, and the short road leading to the incongruous semicircle in the mountain. The actual entry to the facility looked as if it could have been painted by Wile E. Coyote for the Roadrunner, it was such a perfect, bland hole.

Above and to the right of that black entrance was an ancient fissure in the rock, complete with straggling trees clinging desperately to the vertical edges. The picture must have been taken in the springtime, because there were still traces of snow here and there. Kinsey wondered if the crack was part of the geological fault present in the mountain.

Other photographs purported to show scenes inside the actual complex. Intent men and women seated at computers, their faces underlit by green and red illumination, looking up at a giant display of unintelligible graphics on the wall. A tunnel carved out of raw rock, with a forklift proceeding on its mysterious way. The obligatory "We Track Santa Claus Every Christmas" display—the Cub Scouts were very superior about that one. And of course, the photographs of the current command, with U.S.

and Canadian generals posed pointedly beneath their respective flags.

Beside Kinsey, Bert Samuels sat with his fingers laced over his belly and a smirk on his face.

The audience was beginning to get restless; the Border collie had herded her charges into the second row of seats, behind the intent men, and they were beginning to pop up and down again. She was starting to get angry with them when a tall young man in uniform stepped onto the stage. This managed to attract the kids' attention. He favored them with a small smile. One of the boys yipped, "Captain! He's a captain, see he has those bars on his shoulder."

The captain cleared his throat, and if by magic, the audience calmed down. "Yes, you're right," he said. "I'm a captain in the United States Air Force. My name is Dave Weikman, and I'm here to tell you all about Cheyenne Mountain Operations Center, or as we call it, CMOC. CMOC contains elements from NORAD, USSPACECOM, and AFSPC. You may have noticed that the military tends to talk in alphabet soup."

The Cub Scouts giggled. The cooing-and-billing couple in the corner had taken a break and were listening, too—definitely spies. The coterie frowned. Definitely former military, Kinsey thought. No sense of humor at all.

"What all those letters mean is 'North American Aerospace Defense,' 'United States Space Command,' and 'Air Force Space Command.' Of course there's a Navy and Army Space Command too that's part of USSPACECOM. All of us together exist to give the President early warning of missile attacks—"

"Space aliens like in *Star Wars*?" one of the Cub Scouts asked. "Cool!"

Captain Weikman grinned. "Just like *Star Wars*." He shared the joke with the rest of the audience, most of whom, Kinsey noticed, didn't get it. Or at least didn't appreciate it.

"We also track leftover space junk, such as obsolete satellites or even tools the astronauts might have lost during space walks. We wouldn't want one of those to come streaking through the atmosphere and have the Russians or the Chinese mistake it for a missile. And of course you all know that every year we track the progress of Santa Claus from the North Pole."

The adults grinned. The Cub Scouts groaned, clearly disappointed that the captain thought they still believed in Santa Claus.

"Now, unlike what you might have seen in the movies, we can't actually launch a nuclear attack from CMOC—"

"Then it's not really aerospace *defense*, is it?" one of the older men challenged. "Why'd you call it that?"

Unfazed, Weikman nodded. "Excellent point, sir. When Cheyenne Mountain was first established, back in the sixties, we actually did have an active role in—"

Kinsey sighed and closed his eyes. There was nothing here he couldn't find in some concentrated Web-surfing. Weikman wrapped up the briefing with a quick question-and-answer period, mostly about what it was like to work in the Mountain. The captain was suitably vague about the number of people involved, and Kinsey could hear a snort of derision from his escort. However many there were, some were Canadians and many lived in Fort Carson, the base at the foot of Cheyenne Mountain. How utterly *fascinating*, Kinsey thought.

Once the captain was finished, the uniformed escort stepped forward again, moving the tourists along in a not-too-subtle fashion back to their tour bus. One stopped in front of Kinsey and Samuels. An indecipherable, wordless exchange between the two military men resulted in the enlisted man moving on, leaving the other two alone in the room.

Moments later they were rejoined by Weikman. "Well, gentlemen, I understand that you're supposed to get the full Cook's Tour."

"The what?" Samuels said.

Weikman smiled again, and Kinsey smiled back. Part of it, of course, was sharing the joke that Samuels didn't get; the rest was just responding to the other man's expression. When people smiled, you smiled back. A politician's son learned that sort of thing early. "Just an expression," Kinsey informed Samuels.

Samuels looked skeptical.

"If you'll come this way, I'll take you to the Mountain," Weikman said, and led them out of the Visitors Center to a navy-blue van.

Minutes later, they approached the final checkpoint outside the plain upside-down U that was the entrance to the complex. He verified one more time that he had no recording devices of any kind on his person, no cell phone, no PDA, no camera. He signed off on a form attesting to the fact that he would have to rely solely on his own mortal memory, and fingerprinted it. Then they were back in the van, on the road that led straight to the hole in the mountain, and Weikman kept on going, straight inside, into the dark.

It was dark, of course, only by contrast to the brilliant fall sunshine outside. The walls of the tunnel were smooth and well lighted, but Kinsey couldn't avoid a shudder of claustrophobia, and he found himself breathing more deeply, as if somehow oxygen was consumed by the bones of the mountain around them. Two flatbed trucks loaded with heavy equipment passed them, headed for the outside world. The rumble of the engines echoed long after they were gone.

The sedan traveled perhaps a mile before pulling into a large cavern, the roof vanishing above a network of catwalks and lights. The three men got out, and Kinsey squinted upward, trying to estimate how high the cavern stretched; the lights looked like stars. All around him, people and vehicles moved with purpose and focus. Because of the size of the cavern, even the level of activity around them didn't make the room seem crowded.

Weikman led them to a large office and presented them to "the Joint Command of the Cheyenne Mountain Complex, General Pace and Brigadier Cassidy." They exchanged pleasantries, and the commanders offered him scones and coffee.

"You'll receive our full unclassified briefing booklet before you leave," Pace assured him.

Kinsey smiled politely and thanked him. Bored or not, he was thinking about the story, trying on different angles. He needed a hook, and so far he hadn't seen anything attention-grabbing that would compel a reader to follow along.

"I can handle the tour from here," Samuels told Weikman once they were out of the commander's office.

The captain was in the unpleasant position of attempting to contradict a superior officer who was not by any means in his chain of command. Not that it would be any easier if Samuels *were* in his chain of command, Kinsey thought, grateful that he was a civilian.

Having pushed the issue as far as he dared, Weikman stepped aside, and Samuels turned to gesture to Kinsey. The reporter noted with amusement that Weikman was already picking up a telephone, reporting no doubt to someone else that a lieutenant colonel was running around loose with a civilian reporter in tow.

But, somewhat to his surprise, Samuels followed

the expected protocol. He wasn't allowed to enter any of the control rooms until Samuels notified the occupants that he had an uncleared civilian with him. The radar screens and computer displays were curiously blank. The officers were polite and pleasant and not too obvious about wishing he would go away and let them get back to work.

So he was polite and pleasant back, and asked intelligent questions and found out absolutely nothing new at all.

After the third or fourth such visit, as they headed for yet another intersection of tunnels, Kinsey caught at Samuels' arm.

"All right," he said at last, "what is this all about? It's all fascinating, I'm sure, and if I were writing a history of this place I'd be just thrilled, but really, Samuels, *who cares?* Today's hot stories are *not* tucked away in the systems of a facility that's been around for more than thirty years."

Samuels glanced farther down the corridor, to an elevator guarded by yet another armed guard sitting at a desk, and then smiled at him. "You just have no idea what's in this mountain," he said.

"And I suppose you're going to break security and tell me all about it?" Skepticism dripped from every word.

"I would *never* break security," Samuels said with a show of indignation. "You don't have to be insulting."

"Then why am I here?"

"Maybe your father hoped that you'd see something that piqued your interest." Samuels took a couple of steps farther down the corridor and lowered his voice. Kinsey had to follow in order to hear him.

The jerk was leading him, Kinsey realized. Coaxing him down the hallway toward something Samuels wanted him to see. Something that Samuels couldn't mention directly—because it was classified.

Of all the incredibly stupid situations to be in, Kinsey thought, and how completely typical of his father to set him up this way.

"Naturally, you wouldn't betray anything secret," he jibed. "Even though the public has a right to know."

A shadow crossed Samuels's eyes, as if he were momentarily indecisive. "Classified material doesn't fall into that category," he answered after a pause that was a moment too long. "That's just Need to Know."

"Oh, screw it." Kinsey pushed past Samuels, past the airman seated at the desk, to the elevator door, and pushed the button.

The guard was already getting to his feet, unsnapping his holster, as Samuels, pursued by second thoughts, moved between them. The airman opened his mouth to protest.

The elevator door opened.

The next thing Frank Kinsey knew, the muzzle of a gun was in his ear, someone's arm was around his throat, and he had been pulled into the elevator. The last glimpse he had of Bert Samuels was of the man's shocked face—his mouth opening and closing like a goldfish—through the rapidly closing elevator doors.

CHAPTER EIGHT

"Hey!" As a response to the occasion, it lacked something. Kinsey decided not to get picky. He could always edit the story later, assuming he had the chance. At least now he had his hook. "Hey, I didn't mean to . . ."

The alarms had already started as the elevator doors were sliding shut—he had to give somebody credit for fast response. By contrast, it was very quiet in the elevator itself. He was surprised that power hadn't been cut off, but the little room continued its smooth descent. "Look, I don't want any problems." His mouth was very dry.

"Shut up," the voice behind him said. The arm across his Adam's apple jerked, and Kinsey reached up involuntarily to try to pull it away. The muzzle of the gun nudged warningly at his earlobe. He could hear the harsh rasp of his captor's breathing, smell the tang of beer on his breath. "Just shut up. You're that reporter they're all worried about, aren't you?"

The elevator was still dropping. Kinsey found himself watching the indicator lights, amazed at the number of floors that seemed to be going by. He'd had no idea there was such a deep hole in Cheyenne Mountain.

Meanwhile, several stories above them, Samuels was screaming orders to contact Blue Book, and most of the staff around them, including the airman on guard, were looking at him blankly. Major Weikman, who had been nearby, faded back to pick up a telephone, muttering rapidly to personnel on the other end.

In the elevator, his captor's arm jerked again, demanding the attention it already had. "Aren't you? You were the only one out there in civvies. Being escorted. Touring."

Given the choice between following the order to shut up and answering the question, Kinsey opted for the latter, but kept it brief. "Yes, I am." Worried? Nobody so far had seemed particularly worried about anything, at least not until now. He was willing to make up for the lack all by himself.

"Did that article in *NewsWorld* last month about secrets and the public, right?"

"That was mine." Normally he'd have been very pleased that someone actually remembered his work, recognized his byline. Somehow that reaction didn't seem appropriate now.

"Well, I'll give you secrets," the voice said. "People dying. People getting murdered. We're all gonna die and they aren't gonna tell anybody. I was there. I know."

Despite being dry-mouthed with fear, Kinsey couldn't help feeling a flicker of interest.

"Where?" he said.

His captor unwrapped the arm from around Kinsey's neck and shoved the reporter against the far wall of the elevator. "Wouldn't you like to know?"

"Sure I would," Kinsey gasped, trying to keep from sliding down the wall. The man in front of him was wearing rumpled fatigues, the gold leaves that indicated he was a major, and U.S. insignia. He was also waving around a standard U.S. issue sidearm, but at least it wasn't pointed into Kinsey's ear anymore.

"They said you'd be coming today," the major

muttered. There were flecks of spittle around his lips, and his gaze danced from the indicator lights to the walls of the elevator and back again. "They said. Kinsey. Reporter. You'd be interested in the aliens, wouldn't you? You'd tell them. Somebody has to tell them. We're all gonna die."

Oh, hell. Not aliens. Why'd it have to be aliens? Frank Kinsey made a mental note to write a really scathing exposé of security at domestic military bases, just as soon as he got home. "What aliens?" *Keep him talking. Get him interested. I'll bet they'll be waiting to jump him just as soon as those doors open again.*

"The Goa'uld. They send us through the Gate to find the Goa'uld, but it wasn't them. They're gonna kill us all. We need to tell somebody. Tell the President." For a moment the blue eyes ceased their darting, and the major was looking right at him, confusion uppermost. His gun hand had fallen to his side.

"Who are the Goa'uld? And what's your name?"

"Morley, David, Major, United States Air Force, 993-47-6296." The words came out staccato, as if the man didn't even have to think about them. And of course he didn't: Name. Rank. Serial number.

"Dave Morley? Can I call you Dave?"

The major licked his lips, nodded.

The elevator jolted to a stop, and the gun came up again, pointed unwaveringly at Kinsey.

They were waiting, all right. Six armed personnel, eerily silent, standing in a semicircle around the elevator door, automatic rifles aimed and ready. Kinsey hadn't had this much firepower aimed at him since his last trip to Serbia. He hadn't liked it much then, either, and it had been a lot less personal the last time.

"Get back," Morley said. "Get back or I blow him away. That's an order, dammit."

"They're not taking orders from you right now,

Dave," said a calm, unruffled voice from behind the firing squad. "Why don't you just put that down and we can talk about this."

Kinsey desperately wanted to turn his head and find out who was being so damn cool about this situation, but he was afraid that if he did, he'd miss the exciting picture of Morley firing at him.

"Get back," Morley repeated. "Order them back, O'Neill."

"You know I can't do that," the voice went on reasonably. "Come on, Major, this is a standoff. Put the weapon down."

"Like hell I will." Morley's other hand went to his belt, pulled something free, and brought it to his mouth. "You get back, or I'll blow us all to Kingdom Come." Kinsey could feel the release, but the sensation of the gun in his ear kept him from dashing to safety. That, and the fact that his knees were about to give out on him entirely.

The reasonable voice sighed. "But Dave, that's such a cliché."

Morley rotated his hand to display its contents.

Sure enough, it was a grenade, and the pin was out.

"Back off, people." The voice was reluctant, and just a little less cool than it had been.

"You snipe me off," Morley said, "and the senator's little boy goes with me."

"Would I do a thing like that, Dave?"

"In a heartbeat, O'Neill." Morley stepped forward and grabbed Kinsey's shoulder, shoving him around to face the squad. Kinsey's relief at seeing their weapons lowered was tempered by Morley's arm once again around his throat. Out of the corner of his eye he could see the grenade.

At least now he could also see the owner of the quiet voice, a tall, lean colonel also dressed in fatigues, standing opposite the elevator as if preparing for a *High Noon* confrontation. Behind him, two women, one in a white lab coat and the other a pretty blonde in fatigues, joined a younger man dressed in civilian clothes and a massive specimen with some kind of strange symbol on his forehead. *What kind of tattoo is that? Who's the doctor?* he wondered, his mind scrambling desperately for something to think about other than the armed grenade. Morley must have holstered the gun. That part was good, anyway.

"Come on," the major muttered in his ear.

"Where're you going?" the colonel—O'Neill, Morley had called him—asked pleasantly, as if they were just discussing the weather and plans for the day. The look in his eyes, though, was anything but pleasant. It was hard and angry, and a fresh shudder of terror went through Kinsey at the realization that he was trapped, not just by a crazy man who had gone off the deep end and was waving a live grenade around, but between the crazy and another man who might not be crazy himself but was coldly determined to stop the crazy. Kinsey himself was nothing more than a really annoying obstacle, and O'Neill didn't look like he had much sympathy for obstacles.

I'm a hostage, for God's sake!

Yeah, yeah, yeah, you're a hostage. You're *in the way.*

Morley forced him down the hall, past the squad and the pleasantly glowering colonel, toward yet another door, and then through that into a large room.

A very large room. It soared at least a couple of stories, and there were assorted desks and consoles currently being occupied by staff who slowly realized they'd been invaded. The ripple of information passed from the back of the room to the front, lapping against a metal ramp leading up to a huge round stone circle set on end. He could see the opposite wall through the circle—no, it was a pair of circles, one inside the other. The opening they surrounded was perhaps twice the height of a man.

For an instant Kinsey actually forgot about the grenade. He was definitely in a place where he wasn't supposed to be, seeing things he wasn't supposed to see, and his reporter's instincts were wild to know more, to *find out and tell*. What was this place? What was that thing? What were all these people doing down here? This had definitely not been covered in the NORAD briefing.

He was reminded abruptly as Morley yanked him to one of the consoles. The screen saver showed a series of large squares with cryptic symbols. Kinsey looked from the screen saver to the monument at the top of the ramp and noted several similarities in the carved markings.

He was amazed at his own ability to notice such details at a time like this. But he'd always been that way. Displacement activity, an old girlfriend had informed him once. Rather than think about the threat of the here and now, he noticed stupid details, remembered stupid trivia. She'd been going for a Ph.D. in psychology and had a comma-shaped red mole on her left hip.

O'Neill walked up to stand within arm's length of the major and his hostage. Morley yanked Kinsey around in front of himself as a shield, displaying the grenade as he did so.

"Dave, come on." O'Neill's voice was quiet, reasonable. Not coaxing. Morley would have responded badly to that, Kinsey thought. Coaxing would have sounded too condescending. "Give me the grenade. Let's not do something here that everybody's gonna be sorry for.

"Especially," he added, casting a wry glance at the armed weapon, "me."

"People have to know," Morley said. Kinsey could feel the major relaxing just a little as he lowered his voice to speak directly to O'Neill. "They have a right to know. I'm gonna show them. I'm gonna show *him*"—he jerked his arm around Kinsey's throat—"and he'll tell. That's what he came for, isn't it? So people would know?"

A flash of anger entered O'Neill's eyes and then was gone. "I don't know what he came for, Dave, but it wasn't this. Let the guy go."

Maybe he wasn't just in the way, then. Was that a relief?

Not yet, Kinsey decided.

Morley angled himself to the computer console and used the hand holding the grenade to slam one of the keys on the keyboard. A roar from the stone circle made Kinsey jump, as the inner part of the circle rotated and something clanked into place.

"I knew we should have locked down those things," came a voice from nearby. A woman's voice. Probably the one who'd been standing behind O'Neill in the hallway.

Morley ignored it and hit another symbol. His thumb slipped a little off the grenade plunger and Kinsey could feel the instant tension in the room, and especially in his captor's body, until it was back in place, substituting for the missing pin. Out of the corner of his eye he could see the giant wheel spinning again, like a combination lock, or maybe a roulette wheel. What *was* that thing?

"You didn't believe me," Morley was saying. "You thought I screwed up. But nobody could have pulled those men out, not even you, the mighty O'Neill. I'll show you. I'll show him. I'll show everybody." He hit another symbol.

"Remind me to update our internal security plan," O'Neill said to no one in particular, never taking his eyes off Morley.

The wheel spun.

From somewhere else in the room, a hollow voice said, "Chevron three encoded . . ."

A glimpse of movement above his line of vision made Kinsey look up to see the broad window of an observation room, one story up, overlooking the drama being played out below. Several men in uniform, including at least one general, were watching intently. He wondered if the window would be impervious to the blast of the grenade, or if all the observers would be caught in a lethal shower of glass shards. They didn't seem personally apprehensive—the lucky sods.

He was going to have a *long* talk with his father when he got back.

"Chevron six encoded," said the hollow voice. He realized that he'd been hearing Morley hit more symbols, and the wheel spin—the wheel of fortune? What was behind door number one?—without consciously noting it. O'Neill's lips were thinned with frustration.

Behind him, close to the entrance to the room, Kinsey could see Bert Samuels, looking more than a little panicked. Although why *he* should be panicked was beyond Frank Kinsey at the moment. Samuels wasn't the one with a grenade at his ear.

"I'm going to take him there," Morley was saying. "I'll show him. He's a hotshot combat reporter, isn't he? I recognized you, buddy. And God just dropped you in my lap so we could tell the world. You and me."

Frank swallowed. "What are we going to tell the world, Major?" he asked.

"Come see," Morley said, giggling. "Come see."

"Morley!" O'Neill was making one last effort to play by the rules. "Stop! That's an order!"

"Ah, stick it in yer ear," Morley snickered, and reached for another symbol.

"Wormhole activated!" A cry went up from one of the computer consoles, and a thunderous roar from the giant ring jerked Kinsey's attention around, even away from the grenade. "SG-9 returning!"

He had never seen anything like it, never. His reporter's mind grasped for words, for some way to describe what he was seeing.

If you took a giant wave off Maui, and funneled it into a cylinder, and whooshed it out of a straw . . . if you took the geyser Old Glory and set it on its side . . . you might have an image to work with. It was blue. It wasn't water.

It was light, or plasma, or something, and it vomited forth from the ring at the top of the ramp. Then it swooshed back into itself, but he couldn't see the back wall of the underground room anymore; the plasma stuff had settled into the diameter of the monument like quicksilver covering the surface of a mirror.

"What the *hell*?"

CHAPTER NINE

Things began to happen very, very quickly.

Morley's attention too had been yanked to the phenomenon of the Gate, though Kinsey could have sworn the man was disappointed rather than amazed. At the same time, O'Neill made an accurate, if suicidal, lunge at the grenade.

Before Kinsey could do more than realize what was happening, O'Neill had forced Morley backward against the console, and the armed grenade had fallen from his nerveless hand. Someone else—the blonde?—had leaped in and was applying pin pressure, disarming it again.

It must be, Kinsey thought, a new-model weapon if they could do that. It should have blown them all to Kingdom Come. Modern technology was a wonderful thing.

Then he threw up, and his knees finally gave way completely.

Someone made a noise of utter disgust and pushed him aside.

Someone else grabbed him and moved him along. As his initial nausea receded, he realized that they weren't hauling him out of danger so much as shoving him the hell out of the way. He found a handy back wall and staggered against it, trying to comprehend what he was seeing.

Morley, he was glad to see, was already in restraints.

The giant circle was occluded with shimmering light, and through it came at least a dozen figures in uniform, as if they'd been tossed through, losing their balance on the steel ramp as often as not, supporting comrades who had obviously been wounded. In response, the room was filling with medic teams, under the fierce efficient direction of the brunette in the white lab coat, who seemed to be everywhere at once.

He found his jaw opening and closing as he tried to figure out where all these people had come from. Twisting around, he looked up to the observation window. There was the general, no longer watching him but studying the activity in the room below with no surprise but obvious concern.

The room stank of blood and cordite, echoed with shouts and orders and moans.

Kinsey tried edging toward the door. Bert Samuels scrambled to his side, as if to establish that he'd been there all along.

"All right, Samuels, who are these people and what happened to them?" he said, keeping his voice low. A line of gurneys proceeded out of the big room. Without waiting for either reply or permission, Kinsey followed them, keeping out of the way of the medics supporting IV poles and applying pressure bandages. He could hear Samuels sputtering behind him. Evidently someone had thought that a lieutenant colonel as escort counted as "under confinement," and they were too busy to keep track of one annoying gadfly.

The gadfly in question shortly found himself in the middle of a very busy emergency clinic. They were well set up to handle mass casualties, he noted, and no one seemed shocked or horrified or surprised. The staff behaved as though it were all in a day's bloody work.

So this happened a lot?

Apparently.

Keeping back along the wall, out of the way and beneath he hoped, any kind of notice, he focused on what he was seeing and hearing, wishing he had his camera.

"Ringer's lactate—"

"IV stat—"

"We've got a torn artery here—"

"My God, they're coming—!"

Several of the victims were burned, their uniforms smoking and crisped and gaping to reveal bright-red tissue seeping blood. He had seen similar injuries from grenades, from laser burns. There were very few common, ordinary bullet holes.

"We've got to get out of here," Samuels babbled, tugging on his sleeve. "Come on, we've got to get out of here." The colonel was white and sweating, his voice too high and too loud. "Kinsey, come on. We're not supposed to be in here."

"Damn straight you're not supposed to be in here," came a growl from behind them. Kinsey glanced over his shoulder to see O'Neill standing with one hand on Samuels's arm. "When exactly did you lose your mind, Samuels? I suggest you get out of here and report to the brig. It'll save us all a lot of time." The tall colonel transferred his glare to Kinsey. "You too," he added. "There are people here who need help, and you're in the way."

Kinsey couldn't help but agree, but there was a story here. *Damn*, there was a story here! He tried to get a closer look at the casualties.

He was stopped almost immediately by a giant with a metal tattoo on his forehead.

"You will come with me," the giant said.

"Sure," he answered helplessly. Why not? Right down the rabbit hole.

"Okay, General," Kinsey said a few minutes later, when the dark giant escorted him into the upper observation room. Not, he noted wryly, either Pace or Cassidy; the name tag on the blue uniform identified this man as Hammond, and the deference shown by everyone else in the room placed him at the very top of the hierarchy. Kinsey was not impressed. "Let's get down to it. What's the scoop here? What is that thing and where did those troops come from?"

The general gave him a long, considering stare. All around him other military personnel—staff members—looked uneasily back and forth from the general to the reporter.

"Mr. Kinsey, all of that information is highly classified. You will not be permitted to publish anything whatsoever about what you've seen here today. If you do so, you'll be prosecuted to the full extent of the law. I'll see both you and *Samuels*"—he pronounced the name with special loathing—"rot in jail for the rest of your lives, in solitary confinement if necessary."

"Oh, come now, General. What about the people's right to know? A little thing called the First Amendment?" The words were blithe and brave, but Kinsey was bluffing, and he hated the feeling.

"There's something called overriding national security, as you well know, Mr. Kinsey. And I'd advise you not to push me right now—you're one inch away from being arrested and thrown into the deepest, darkest hole I can find. And you have no idea just how deep and dark that can be."

Kinsey felt his lips skin back from his teeth in what could have been a grimace or a grin. "Threats, General? Now that's a story all by itself. Just how far are you willing to go to protect your little secrets?"

There was a sudden stillness in the room, and Kinsey couldn't quite read the expression that crossed Hammond's face.

And for his part, George Hammond could read all too well what was going on in the reporter's mind. He'd just witnessed the Gate in operation. He'd seen wounded personnel come through what was previously an empty hole, out of nowhere. It was a terrific story, one any reporter would give his eyeteeth to have as an exclusive.

Behind Kinsey, he could see O'Neill appearing in the doorway, shaking his head. The news about the casualties wasn't good, then.

He saw the colonel's gaze shift to Kinsey, standing unknowing before him, and then back to himself. Hammond met O'Neill's eyes, seeing the question that haunted the colonel. His conscience was clear; he had nothing to do with the traffic accident that killed the last reporter who'd gotten too close to the Gate.

It had been a tragedy, of course, but a wonderfully convenient one, and he had felt more than one pang of guilt about his own relief at the man's death.

This time, though, no convenient accident could pull their chestnuts out of the fire. Frank Kinsey was the son of a senator who already knew all about the Stargate, and if anything happened to him "all hell broken loose" would be a pale understatement.

That wouldn't save the reporter from arrest and trial and conviction, of course, but the secret of the Stargate would be royally blown once and for all.

Janet Frasier entered the observation room, ready to report on casualties. Hammond shifted gears with something approaching gratitude. "Mr. Kinsey, I've got more important things to deal with right now than you. You're going to be kept in confinement until I decide exactly what to do with you. Now"—

he took a deep breath and addressed one of the other officers—"get Bert Samuels up here."

Minutes later, a quivering lieutenant colonel stood before him. "S-sir."

The rest of the room was absolutely silent.

No, command was definitely not what it was cracked up to be. Hammond could remember one of his daughters once, in the midst of an impassioned tantrum, calling him a militaristic tyrant who thought he had the power of life and death over everybody around him.

Looking at Bert Samuels, George Hammond almost wished it was true.

The little lieutenant colonel stood at absolute attention, oscillating almost visibly between sheer terror and smirking glee. *Little tattletale,* Hammond thought. Oh, all right, so that wasn't really fair. *Little lickspittle toady. You think your "special relationship" with the Joint Chiefs cuts any ice with me?*

"Mr. Samuels—"

Several of the assembled military involuntarily swallowed at the softness of Hammond's tone. Not one of them missed the deliberate omission of rank.

"—would you mind telling me what on earth possessed you to bring a reporter into this complex?

"And not just into this complex, but into *this* facility?"

"I-I didn't," Samuels stammered. "I mean, I brought him into the complex, but that was at the specific request of Senator Kinsey. His father," Samuels belatedly added, as if it might make a difference. "He, he took matters into his own hands, and then that major grabbed him, and O'Neill—"

Hammond shifted his gaze to target on the line of sweat on Bert Samuels's brow. "So, Colonel, you and Senator Kinsey thought it would be a great idea to have his son do an investigative report on Cheyenne Mountain?"

"It was the senator's idea," Samuels said defensively. Reviewing the circumstances seemed to revive the junior officer's courage. "And this incident is a matter I'm going to have to bring to his attention, sir, since you seem to have a very serious breach of security—"

"I'll bring it to the senator's attention," Hammond agreed. "And to the President's. Your role will be specifically mentioned, I assure you."

Even now the poor airman standing guard at the elevator was being grilled to within an inch of his life, Hammond knew. Kinsey would never have reached the elevator had Morley not grabbed him. That made no difference now; he would have to find a way to soothe an enraged father, already antagonistic to the whole project, as well as justify the facility's response to the President.

"Report, Doctor?"

Standing at attention beside Samuels and reeking of distaste, Janet Frasier kept her face impassive. "We have Major Morley in restraints," she summarized. "The personnel from SG-9 are under care. Five are in critical condition. We haven't been able to get any information from them at this time."

Hammond raised a hand. "That's all right, Captain. I'd appreciate it if you'd let me know if anything changes on that front. Dismissed."

Frasier snapped a salute, executed a parade turn, and marched out.

Hammond shifted his attention back to the quivering Samuels.

"You are not to report anything whatsoever to the senator unless and until I specifically authorize it. I have *that* authority direct from the President of the United States. Are you clear on that, Colonel?"

Samuels shrank into himself. It was almost a shame to send him away, Hammond thought. It was so interesting to watch the man change colors. He would have liked to watch some more, but he needed to pass along the casualty information first. He could always have a whole series of little talks with the man.

"Yes, sir," he gulped.

No matter how you cut it, it was a gawdawful mess. And he knew who the senator would take it out on.

Hammond had never been so close to losing his own rank in his long and spotless military career, and that realization was the only thing that was keeping him from flaying Samuels alive.

He would save that pleasure for later, he promised himself, no matter how this debacle turned out.

"You're dismissed, Colonel. I want you to return to house arrest. You are to have *no* communication with *anyone* without my personal authorization. Sergeant, escort the colonel to the holding facility. I'll be in my office. Notify me immediately of any changes to this situation."

"Yes sir," the attendant multitudes chorused, and Hammond swept out, borne by a wave of absolute fury, not least at himself. He should have realized in the morning's meeting that Morley was going to snap, should have ordered him to report to Dr. Frasier immediately. She'd been concerned. But no, he'd had to let the boy find his own way, and now—

He was more concerned about Morley than he was about the reporter, of course. Morley was one of *his*, and he'd never let something like this happen to one of his men before, even under combat conditions. Hammond sat in the leather chair behind the desk and swiveled around, resting his fingertips on the desk pad and leaning back to organize his thoughts.

It was a very clean desk, the surface bare of all but the essentials: the desk pad, two telephones, a pen laid neatly to one side.

The first thing was to call the President and report

the incident. He prided himself on using the direct-line red phone very rarely indeed, and then only for major issues.

"Major" issues. He winced. Well, this certainly qualified.

And then he'd have to call the senator and tell *him* what happened.

Maybe he'd get lucky and the President would tell him to keep a lid on it.

The odds of that were less than zero. An isolationist administration, intent on placating a powerful senator, wouldn't dare keep such information to itself.

And what about his opposite numbers? Would Cassidy and Pace want to know what happened to their famous visitor? He could stonewall them, but the senator would roust their turf too, and there would go his security firewall, shot to hell and gone.

And maybe that was the whole idea of sending the reporter here in the first place.

He was going to *eviscerate* Bert Samuels.

But first things first. He reached for the red telephone. There was no need to dial a number; only one connection would be made on this line.

The voice at the other end sounded just like every sound bite it had ever made.

"Mr. President," General Hammond said, "we have a situation . . ."

"Don't blame this on us," Pace said crisply, quite some time later. "Bert Samuels has always had full access to your area. His visit was properly cleared, and he observed all the protocols. Under our agreement, you're responsible for your own bailiwick, George."

"And that gentleman who took him hostage was one of yours, too," Cassidy said genteely. The speakerphone made his voice sound a bit tinny, but Hammond could hear the distinct click of a cup being placed on a saucer. "Seems you might have a bit of cleaning up to do in your own house, George. In fact, we might have some questions about the threat your people pose to *our* security. Do they go crazy a lot in your patch?"

"Thank you, gentlemen," Hammond grated.

He paused for a long moment, trying to think of something else to say, before giving up and replacing the telephone gently in its cradle. It wasn't hard to detect a certain so-*there* tone in Pace's voice—resentment, probably, that a mere lieutenant colonel could go places that were barred to the ostensible CinC of the Cheyenne Mountain Complex. Pace could be justified—barely—in believing that Samuels had obtained the proper clearances to allow his guest into Stargate Command, just as he had in order to allow Kinsey into the Complex to begin with. It certainly wasn't Pace's problem, or Cassidy's.

Of course, it had to be Cassidy who pointed out exactly which emperor was naked. Hammond hoped the Canadian got tea leaves stuck in his very proper mustache.

His eyes moved over the stack of printouts that Major Rusalka and Captain Randolph had produced, with brief summaries.

"Get me Jack O'Neill," he said into the empty air.

Silence answered.

Snarling, Hammond slapped an intercom key on his phone and repeated the order.

CHAPTER TEN

"So this is what you were trying to maneuver me into seeing," Kinsey said absentmindedly, mentally trying on leads for size. He couldn't dictate how the headlines would read, of course, but he could certainly make suggestions. "The Real Secrets of Space Defense"—nah, too tabloid. "The Ring of Death"— oh, forget it, let the editors worry about it. He'd just write the story. The story of a lifetime. He wondered briefly if his father had known, and then smirked. Of course the old man had known. He wanted this cover blown. Well, he was going to get his wish. There's never been a story like this one before, never.

Of course, he'd have to get more information. "What *is* that thing? A transdimensional portal?" Nobody would go for that. He needed pictures. No, he needed somebody to come forward and swear to it under oath; pictures were too easy to fake, even motion pictures could be altered with special effects.

"No," Samuels said. "That is, I can't confirm or deny that. Or anything. Oh God. I need to talk to the senator. To General Wickersham. Somebody."

"Wickersham? Oh yeah, your boss at the Pentagon. Doe he know about this?" Kinsey was making a mental list of potential interviewees. This one could go all the way to the top. "Dad, of course. He knew about this all along. He cooked this up just so I could see what was going on—does he have something against these guys or something? It's a great story—"

"It's *not* a story, it's classified, you can't publish anything," Samuels babbled. "No. No. You'll go to jail. *I'll* go to jail!"

"What, not even how I spent a lazy afternoon at the Cheyenne Mountain Complex looking over the latest stuff at U.S. Space Command?" Kinsey's gaze sharpened. "It'll knock the transportation industry right on its ass—Oh will you just shut up about the going-to-jail part? You wanted me to see this stuff, right? That's why you brought me here to begin with!"

"You weren't supposed to actually *see*—we just thought you'd be curious, scare Hammond—"

Kinsey snorted. "Hammond? This is George Hammond, right? I thought I recognized him. From what I've heard, it would take more than one reporter to scare George Hammond. Hmmmmm. I should go back and take another look at his service record. I wonder how long this has been going on . . ."

"Let me out of here!" Samuels yelled, pounding on the door. "I want to talk to General Wickersham! It wasn't my fault!"

Jack O'Neill sat across the table from his commanding officer, staring at a point just past Hammond's right ear.

"If you have any suggestions, Colonel, I'm open to hearing them," Hammond was saying.

There's always an "accident," O'Neill thought, but quashed that idea immediately. He respected Hammond more than any other commanding officer he'd ever had, not least because the general made it very clear that he was always, no matter what, an instrument of legal, constitutionally authorized policy. George Hammond would have no part of assassination. It wasn't in the nature of the man, and O'Neill had always considered himself a good judge of character.

Still, he couldn't forget the look in the eyes of another reporter, dying on a Washington street, telling him with his last breath that his death was O'Neill's fault. Hammond would not countenance such action, but someone would. There were too many people out there who appealed to a "higher moral position" and used it as an excuse for lying, stealing, even murder.

O'Neill knew with gut certainty that he had to find a way to shut Kinsey up.

"I don't know, sir," he said slowly. "What's the senator trying to do, play chicken with us? I didn't think he was on good terms with his son. Why send him to uncover something about the Stargate project and publish it?"

"Senator Kinsey still thinks God is on our side," Hammond muttered. "Using his own son that way would appeal to his twisted little mind."

O'Neill's lips twisted, remembering the Mom-and-apple-pie speech that the senator had used to try to deny the imminent threat of the Goa'uld.

"God's on the side of the heavy artillery, and at the moment that's Goa'uld," he responded, and he and the general shared a wry smile. "But he couldn't predict Morley's going Section Eight."

"The trouble is, we can't arrest him for violating the Official Secrets Act until he actually *does* it. Too many people would want to know why." Hammond scanned the articles and summaries one more time.

"If he's anything like his father—"

"He's not," the general interrupted. "He and his father are usually, very publicly, on the outs as far as politics goes, and the man's reporting on other subjects has been fairly balanced. Maybe he could be convinced." His fingers brushed the sheaf of papers before him, and his eyes narrowed thoughtfully. "He did some nice work on Kosovo. He's done a spy story, too, about the damage done by some of the DOE leaks to the Chinese. He doesn't seem to represent his father's views at all."

O'Neill nodded. "But there's that article about secrecy—he's for more declassification, not less. And he actually saw the casualties, General. We lost three men from SG-3, and six more are in at least serious condition. He's going to want some explanation." He shook his head as another thought occurred to him. "If Kinsey and his father aren't on good terms, why would the senator send him here?"

"Peace offering, maybe. Tantalize him with a good story. Who knows." Hammond stared at the papers again. Nope, not what it was cracked up to be—and he'd better be right this time.

He'd liked the young man. He'd handled being a hostage well; no automatic threats to sue, just an endless need to know. Rather like Carter's, or Dr. Jackson's.

Which was not at all the military need to know, of course.

But the decision was his to make. His and no one else's.

"This Frank Kinsey has been in a war zone," he said slowly. "He seems to understand what war is about. He's against unnecessary secrets, but maybe he understands the necessary ones.

"Colonel, perhaps you ought to show him what *this* war is all about."

"*Sir?*"

It did give Hammond an unholy pleasure to know that he could still catch his maverick officer totally off guard.

"You heard me. We don't want him to write about us, but if we don't give him something he's never going to leave us alone. I know the type. So let's show him what we're up against and try to convince him we've got a legitimate need to slap 'Top Secret' all over it. I know you're not happy with Morley's story about what happened on Etaa. Neither am I. But whatever it was, the Jaffa ought to be gone by now. It should be safe. Take him through, Jack."

O'Neill, still flummoxed, stood up. His expression made it clear he thought his commander had completely lost his mind. "Ohhhhh-kay. I'll go talk to him. Maybe that will give me some ideas. But I *really* don't think this is a good idea, sir."

Hammond smiled, as if being a general gave him a special insight and certainty that everything would work out just fine.

"Just don't let him get bruised, all right? I'd rather not explain that to his father." He was already beginning to wonder the same thing his subordinate was, but he wasn't going to back down now. He gave the orders, by God. He made the decisions, right or wrong. That was what he was paid for.

"Oh, no. This is a very, very, very bad idea." Jackson was shaking his head adamantly.

It wasn't necessarily the reaction O'Neill had expected from the scientist. "Not that I'm arguing with you, but why?" He'd called his team together in his office; Devorah Randolph was standing by, listening, making lists.

Sam Carter was still pale and shaking from the incident with the grenade. "You *know* what will happen if he publishes!"

"If we release the information that there's a genuine alien threat out there, the world's gonna go crazy. You'll have cultists worshiping the Goa'uld, you'll have the idiots who think we've already sold out, you'll have the worst idiots like the senator thinking we can beat them with one hand tied behind our back, you'll have the ones who actually *are* trying to sell out—" Jackson leaned back in his chair, ticking off the world's responses on his fingers.

Teal'C was listening, fascinated. "You are saying that your world would not immediately unite to defeat an alien threat that intends to destroy you all?"

The rest of the team just stared at him.

"You can take that as a 'no,' Teal'C," O'Neill said dryly. "I think what Hammond wants is for us to try to convince Frank Kinsey of that."

"Do you think we *can*?" Carter wanted to know.

"We're going to give it our best shot. And if we take any reporter anywhere, it's probably better that it be Etaa, because once the Jaffa set their trap and collected the people there, there's no reason for them to hang around. At least we won't have to worry about the senator's little boy getting himself killed."

Randolph, sitting in a corner, listened hard and added "vests, bulletproof, five (5) ea.," to her list.

O'Neill barely noticed the decor of the small office currently serving as a holding room for Samuels and Kinsey. He'd spent his adult life in the military version of interior decorating, and it held no particular horrors for him.

It was clear that Frank Kinsey didn't share that sentiment. The reporter was on his feet immediately as O'Neill came into the room. The door was shut firmly behind the colonel by an armed airman, and the reporter's eyes widened at the sight. Obviously he'd known the door was locked, but that was all.

Samuels, on the other hand, wasn't surprised in the least. He too was on his feet and talking. "Look, O'Neill, you've got to let me talk to General Wickersham. This situation isn't my fault—who was that madman, anyway? I demand you let me out of here."

O'Neill gave him a withering glance. "Sit down and shut up, Bert. That's an order, in case you've forgotten."

Samuels opened his mouth to continue talking, and O'Neill tilted his head inquiringly. "You didn't hear me?"

Mouth shut, Samuels sank into a chair and began wringing his hands. Silently.

"Don't try that with me, Colonel," Kinsey said. "I'm not in your chain of command."

"I'm aware of that, Mr. Kinsey." O'Neill studied the other man, looking for resemblances to his father. Thankfully, they were few. Kinsey was in his late twenties or early thirties, in good physical condition but with a hairline already receding. He stood well balanced on the balls of his feet, as if ready to move in any direction. Some martial arts training, O'Neill diagnosed. But no signs of the family insanity. Yet.

"Why don't you sit down and tell me what you think you saw today, Mr. Kinsey?" he invited, seating himself on the edge of a desk.

"Stick around and you'll read it in the Sunday paper."

O'Neill allowed himself a small smile. "Maybe. But you want to make sure you've got the story straight, don't you? I'm sure you've got questions."

Samuels squeaked. O'Neill pointedly ignored him.

"I'm sure you wouldn't answer those questions with a gun to your head," Kinsey replied, but he took a chair and swiveled around to study the colonel. "O'Neill. Jack O'Neill. I remember hearing about you. You've seen some action, haven't you?"

"Here and there." Combat fatigues didn't lend themselves to the ribbons, medals, and lettuce of honors and commendations, thank God.

"You were a POW for a while, weren't you?"

O'Neill shrugged. "Neither here nor there, is it?"

"Maybe. I heard you retired some time ago—after your kid died—"

O'Neill controlled the muscles of his jaw with an

effort, but Kinsey must have seen something anyway. "I'm sorry about that, by the way."

O'Neill acknowledged the condolence with an infinitesimal tilt of the head.

"So why'd you unretire? Or did you ever retire in the first place?"

"There was some work to do," O'Neill said vaguely.

"Work here?"

"Among other places. It's not a perfect—world."

Kinsey laughed. "Okay. You want questions, real questions? How's this for starters?

"Who's the nutcase who grabbed me?

"Where'd he take me?

"What's that ring thing?

"Where'd those people come from?

"What happened to them?

"That's a good start, I think."

O'Neill crossed one leg over the other and drummed his fingers lightly against the desk. "Yeah, I'd call that a pretty good start." After a moment to organize his thoughts, he went on, "The man who took you hostage is Major David Morley. Major Morley has served with distinction for several years, but has had some—difficult—experiences. He was suffering a flashback. We failed to recognize the full extent of the stress he was under, and we offer you our sincere apologies."

"You grabbed that grenade, didn't you?" Kinsey said thoughtfully. "I guess I should thank you. You saved my life."

"Mine too," O'Neill pointed out. "And I think somebody else actually grabbed the weapon, I just knocked it out of his hand." *Thank God for Carter*, he told himself.

"Still." Kinsey drew a deep breath. "Okay, I'll accept that for the time being. Now what about the rest of my questions?"

O'Neill sighed. "I'm afraid you've inadvertently stumbled on a highly classified location, Mr. Kinsey—"

"Call me Frank," the reporter invited, smiling.

Sure, we'll just be buddies! O'Neill thought. "Okay, Frank." *At least I won't have to gag over that last name.* "And you can call me Jack." He smiled as if the two of them really were on the way to becoming friends. "Nonetheless. I'm afraid I can't reveal classified information."

"Oh, come on, *Jack*. I know what I saw. That ring thing spun around and something came out of it, and then people came out of it. Troops. And there wasn't anyplace for them to come *from*. So what is it, a portal of some kind? Where did those guys come from? What happened to them? They saw some action somewhere."

"You were under considerable stress," O'Neill suggested gently. "You may have misinterpreted what you thought you saw."

"Bull puckey," Kinsey snapped. "I know what I saw. I've seen troops coming out of combat—I was in Chechnya and Iraq and Kosovo. If you've got a way to transport men and materiel through some kind of ring thing, the people have a right to know. This could revolutionize trade, transportation, war—" He stopped, looking at the other man appraisingly. "You can even use it to go into space, can't you? We don't have to worry about shuttles blowing up anymore. My God, O'Neill, what *are* you people doing here? And how long have you been doing it?"

There was a very long pause indeed as O'Neill studied Kinsey, looking hard for whatever it was that Hammond had seen in him. "We're fighting a war," he said at last. "And we can't tell anyone, for the same reason that you can't yell 'fire' in a crowded theater. What do you think would happen if you published an article about what you saw here?

Where do you think you *could* publish it—*News of the World*? Either your credibility would be destroyed, or even worse—"

"People might believe me." Kinsey studied him in return. "War? With aliens?"

"Yep."

There was a small, deep silence. Not even Samuels made a sound.

"Shouldn't you have notified every government in the world? What makes you think you can do this all by yourself?"

O'Neill smiled. "What do you think would happen? Extrapolate, Frank. Let's say you personally notify the governments of China, Russia, Iraq, North Korea, France, and Argentina that the U.S. has managed to contact hostile aliens? What are they going to say?"

Kinsey thought about that, imagined the response. Outright disbelief. And if they could convince the world that it was actually true, the accusations that the U.S. had sold out the rest of the planet. The attempts to make advantageous deals for single countries. The hysteria and panic. The skeptics versus the converted. "Ouch," he murmured.

O'Neill nodded. "You could say that."

The reporter took a deep breath. "But how do I know any of this is true? How do I know it isn't just an elaborate cover for some new U.S. technology?"

"There's a switch. Usually the aliens get all the credit. I don't suppose you'd be willing to take my word for it."

"Um, no." With the air of a man mustering a last argument, he went on, "If Earth really does have a way to the stars, don't its people have a right to know? And if there are casualties, and a threat to Earth, don't its people have a right to know that, too?"

O'Neill nodded. "And do they have a need to

know? What would they do with the information if they had it? What about that crowded theater?"

Kinsey shook his head in disgust. "Do they have a *'need to know'* that they might die tomorrow? Come on! If the theater's really on fire, they sure as hell need to know! How else can they defend themselves?"

"That's exactly what we're trying to figure out. Until we do—given how the rest of the world will probably react—*should* they know? Would their knowing help or hinder? And would they actually even *want* to know?"

"I would," Kinsey said instantly. "God, aliens? Space travel? Hell, yes, I'd want to know!"

If we don't give him something he's never going to leave us alone. I know the type. . . . Take him through, Jack.

Oh, well. At least they were going to be able to figure out what Dave Morley wasn't telling them.

"Okay," he said. "How'd you like to go for a little ride?"

"A ride?" The reporter was momentarily confused.

"But you can't *do* that!" Bert Samuels squeaked.

CHAPTER ELEVEN

Most of the people who worked at the Cheyenne Mountain Complex were support personnel. They had a regular schedule, eight to five, five days a week. The rest, of course, were on rotating shifts, keeping the radar sweeps manned twenty-four hours a day, seven days a week, looking for Things falling from the sky.

Still, there was a noticeable increase in traffic on NORAD Road heading toward the base and Colorado Springs every Friday just after five o'clock.

George Hammond had made sure that Bert Samuels was right in the middle of that traffic, with orders to keep his mouth shut under pain of court-martial and remain at the base BOQ until further notice. He'd spent a good thirty minutes on the phone with Mike Wickersham at the Pentagon, commiserating with him about unruly subordinates who were rapidly accumulating black marks on their service records but still managed to have friends in high places. The military was supposed to be separate from politics. Fat chance.

Hammond himself had stayed late on this particular Friday, doing paperwork, avoiding the traffic, and determinedly not second-guessing himself about this whole harebrained idea. He trusted his instincts about people, and his instincts told him that Frank

Kinsey was a very different man than his father was. He would use reason. He would do the right thing.

He'd better.

The team would go back to Etaa as soon as it had the logistics set up, which meant as soon as Devorah Randolph finished the party for her kids and could come back to work on the weekend. The inconsequential delay added some assurance that whatever had gone wrong on that world would be long gone by the time they got there.

Meanwhile, Frank Kinsey was sequestered in the cold depths of SGC, pestering everyone he could with questions about the Gate. Mostly this meant medical personnel, as he was taken there almost immediately and sequestered in an exam room, away from the casualty ward.

He grilled Janet Frasier as she gave him a complete physical, making sure there were no preexisting conditions that a litigious journalist could blame on the military after going on a mission. Not knowing for sure what she could say and what she couldn't, Frasier said nothing, but kept her probes safely stored in the refrigerator until called for.

"How many people do you get coming through here in a month?" Kinsey asked, pulling a paper sheet up around his hips as he sat on the examining table.

Frasier gave him a pleasant, meaningless professional smile and rapped perhaps a little harder than necessary at the tendon immediately below Kinsey's right knee.

"What kind of injuries to they have?"

"We get a lot of really nasty paper cuts," she murmured, cracking a good one at the left knee for good measure.

"Those men I saw earlier didn't have paper cuts," Kinsey insisted, leaning forward as far as possible to try to peer out the door and into the ward across the hall. "Hey! What's that needle for?"

"Tetanus," she said sweetly, and jabbed. "You know. For lockjaw."

Meanwhile, the SG-1 team was caucusing, trying to figure out how much to say and when. It was very odd to be trying to decide what to *say*, rather than what *not* to say.

"He'll need to know the historical background," Daniel Jackson was saying. "That might actually work in our favor—he'll think we're all a bunch of von Danikens."

"We *are* a bunch of von Danikens," O'Neill pointed out.

Carter and Teal'C exchanged identical glances of bewilderment.

"Before your time," the colonel informed Carter. "Before yours, too, Daniel. How'd you know about him?"

Daniel grinned. "I did an undergraduate paper on the utter implausibility of the idea that aliens had ever visited Earth and created the basis for Egyptian culture, built the pyramids, or gave the Pharaohs their religion."

The rest of them burst out laughing. Even Teal'C's habitual frown lifted for an instant.

"Hey, I got an A-plus on that paper," Daniel said with mock indignation. "The professor said it was the best one he'd ever seen. Wanted me to publish it."

"Well, you can't argue with science," O'Neill said with mock gravity. "And you were *almost* right. They stole from us instead of vice versa."

"Anyway." Carter got up and refilled her coffee cup, adding some powdered almond cream flavoring and ignoring the disgusted looks she got from the others as a result. If they really thought it was that terrible, she reasoned, why did the stuff appear next to O'Neill's coffeepot mere days after he'd found out she liked it? "What about the physics involved? I mean, are we going to give him a complete briefing? That would take days."

"Months," Jackson agreed, scooting his chair aside to let her get back to her own. "But I thought the whole idea was to convince him that he shouldn't be writing about this stuff at all. So why tell him anything? Send him away with an axe hanging over his head."

O'Neill sighed. "First, because Daddy is a senator who already knows too much and doesn't like us. Second, he's got this fixation about the Constitution and the First Amendment, which normally I'd sympathize with but at the moment is really inconvenient, so we're trading information for silence. And third, and most important, because Hammond told us to. I think he's nuts, but he's a general, so . . ." He sighed. "The question is not whether, but how much we tell him. I figure we might as well go for broke. He can't write about anything at all, so we may as well answer all his questions."

"And this is somehow going to *prevent* him from plastering it over every front page in the world?" Jackson was still skeptical.

"Hammond thinks so." O'Neill shrugged. "Right now, I'm more interested in figuring out what went wrong on Etaa. I keep thinking there's more that Morley didn't tell us."

Dave Morley was currently under sedation and in restraints under Frasier's direct supervision. He wasn't telling anyone anything.

Now it was Carter's turn to shrug. "The Jaffa came, they saw, they conquered. They've done it before. Just because we didn't have any prior indication they'd come, doesn't make any difference—we learned that a long time ago. What else could it be?"

"That's the problem. We don't *know* 'what else.' And I keep having this creepy feeling that with all his talking about force fields, he wasn't thinking about Jaffa at all."

"The Goa'uld have long had personal fields, and larger fields they use for their ships," Teal'C pointed out. "It is not unreasonable to suppose they have developed a large, portable field capable of trapping the enemy as in a net."

"That wouldn't exactly be a force field, though," Carter argued. "The technology to fend objects off isn't necessarily related to the technology of trapping people so they can't move."

"I did not say it was. But having developed the one indicates that they could be able to develop the other."

"Okay, okay." O'Neill raised his hand. "Enough. I'm willing to stipulate that the field Dave described actually exists, which means we'd better be on the lookout for it just in case the place isn't completely deserted. If we're lucky, we'll be able to locate some of Shostoka'an's people and we can ask them what the hell happened. In fact, that's probably our best bet."

"They're not going to think much of us as allies if the Jaffa just got through cleaning them out," Carter muttered. "There many not be anybody left. It wasn't that large a population to begin with."

O'Neill closed his eyes. Carter *always* argued.

But she also knew—usually—how to take a hint that her superior was getting exasperated, so she shut up without finishing her thought.

"I don't know about you," O'Neill said, "but I'm going to go home, eat dinner, and go to bed. Tomorrow's likely to be a really, really long day."

"Like today wasn't?"

O'Neill glared. But Carter *had* managed to field that grenade, so he left it at that.

*   *   *

Frank Kinsey was served dinner in his quarters that night, a decent—last?—repast of pork chops, spinach, applesauce, salad, coffee, and even ice cream for dessert. They left him with a briefing manual that he understood to be standard material for new personnel joining the Stargate team. Between that and the TV set tuned exclusively to CNN, he was expected to entertain himself for the evening. He didn't have to hear the soft click to know that he was locked in.

The TV made a comforting stream of background noise as he paged through the manual. Most of them, he noted without surprise, focused on tactics—what information would be available to a team and how they could use it. Apparently "probes" were sent through the Gate to gather data before actual living people went through—a precaution he approved of, but one which didn't always work, judging from the shape those soldiers had been in coming back.

The books also noted that "Before any teams are sent through the Gate, the existence of a DHD on the target site is *always* verified ahead of time. Return to base must be originated from destination. Teams cannot return through a passage originating on the base." A DHD, he gathered, was the mechanism used to open the—passage?—between two predetermined points. The notation had an air of "learned *that* one the hard way." He also noted with amusement the discreet reference about returning "to base" rather than "to Earth."

And apparently one passage couldn't be opened on top of another, which explained Morley's frustration when that other team came back, interrupting him before he could finish opening the Gate himself. Kinsey wondered where he would be right now if Morley had succeeded in putting in all the proper codes to open the Gate first. A new world? The book didn't say.

"Teams are cautioned to send the iris signal before entering the passage for return. If the signal is not sent, the iris on the base Gate will not be opened. Each member of the team will be equipped with a signaling device."

He wasn't sure what that meant, so he filed it away in his ever-increasing store of Questions to Be Asked.

As he read, he listened with half an ear to the steady stream of news. China was still upset over the bombing of its embassy and its loss to the Americans in women's soccer, and still indignant that anyone could possibly believe they had needed to steal nuclear miniaturization technology from the United States. The Patchen Lama had measles. The Euro was down against the dollar and the Common Market was contemplating trade sanctions against the United States. Russia had publicly requested that Washington butt out of the latest India-Pakistan crisis. There were more rumors about AIDS being deliberately imported to black communities in California. Unemployment on the Lakota reservation officially hit 86 percent. Mir's orbit continued to degrade. Islamic fundamentalists in Indiana were taking exception to efforts by Christian fundamentalists to convert them. A world's record opal had been discovered by a three-year-old boy in Australia. A Nazi war criminal had just died in Argentina. Drug terrorists continued efforts to bring down the government of Colombia. Seventeen died in an airplane crash in Indonesia.

O-bla-dee, o-bla-da. Don't they have any idea what's out there? Kinsey wondered, glancing over at the neatly folded fatigues set out on the desk, with boots lined up precisely under them and a cap resting on top. He was reasonably sure that this uniform, unlike the one he'd been issued long ago when he'd done his own military service, would actually fit. *Why do they spend all their time squabbling with each other like a bunch of spoiled brats, when there's a whole universe out there?*

Because they don't know. And I'm going to be the one to tell them.

A cold shiver of delight ran up his spine. Talk about the scoop of the century! And it was going to be his, all his. They'd know the name Kinsey forever. It would be in all the history books—the man who revealed the truth about the stars. Who unified Earth.

Castro denounced the United States for further attempts to assassinate him.

Survivalists in northern Nevada were in the fifteenth day of standing off local and federal law enforcement personnel, claiming that God had declared them a sovereign country.

The FBI and the U.S. Navy apologized for their rush to judgement over the explosion aboard the *Iowa*, while refraining from naming anyone specifically responsible for the rush in the first place.

Three Israelis were arrested in New York for spying on the Lebanese delegation to the UN.

Life on Earth went on, blissfully self-absorbed.

Frank Kinsey hugged himself and paged through briefing books on life in outer space.

CHAPTER TWELVE

Still, when Jack O'Neill led their little party up the ramp to the shimmering pool that was the Stargate, Kinsey abruptly couldn't believe they were serious. If he hadn't seen, less than twenty-four hours before, with his own eyes, real human beings stumble out of that circle, he wouldn't have come anywhere near that maelstrom of blue energy. He was still jumpy from the very sound of it; as soon as the bodiless voice intoned, "Chevron seven encoded; Gate activated," it had *roared* open. Or not exactly "open"— he couldn't see through the Gate anymore. It didn't look like something one *could* walk through. It was as if whatever lay beyond the Gate was pressing against it, as if the Gate were a dam holding it back, and when the iris opened and the portal was activated, it gushed through and then settled back into equilibrium.

He had serious doubts about the sanity of the first person to actually walk through that thing.

But they were looking at him with exaggerated patience, that look that said *We know you're scared but we're too polite to say so*, and so he gritted his teeth and marched after them.

It wasn't fair, really. The four of them were loaded for bear, with rifles and sidearms and all manner of wicked things, and all *he* had was a set of borrowed fatigues. No cameras, no tape recorders. Though he noticed enviously that both Carter and Jackson carried camcorders—so records did exist, and maybe under the Freedom of Information Act—

O'Neill went first. As he touched the surface his body seemed to disappear, as if he were walking into a pool of mercury. He was followed immediately, without hesitation, by the blond Major Samantha Carter. As they disappeared, technicians at the foot of the ramp were doing hasty last-minute checks of the supplies on the transport that would be going with them. It was a cute little mini-tank with treads almost as large as it was, an all-terrain vehicle built for worlds other than Terra. Someone had stenciled F.R.E.D. on its side. It probably stood for something; yet another question to be asked. But not right now. Right now an opaque shimmering mirror awaited him.

The others were waiting for him to go next—Jackson made a little bow and an *After you, Alphonse* gesture, while the tall black guy, Teal'C they called him, simply stood waiting, holding a long staff, a modern-day Roman centurion in battle fatigues. Teal'C always looked like he was frowning mightily, but that seemed to be nothing more than the way his features had settled on his face.

He was going to tell the world about this. *Humanity's Gate to the stars stands in lonely grandeur at the top of a metal ramp that rings beneath the booted feet of—*

The future and fame awaited. So he took a deep breath and held it and followed where O'Neill and Carter had led, into the mystery.

And found himself gasping, tumbling, falling, through a live, twisting, writing tunnel of blue light. It was *cold*, much colder even than the interior of the mountain. He had never felt such cold, sinking icy fangs deep into his bones and not letting go. He couldn't see the others. He knew he had walked into *some*thing, but once in it he lost all sense of sight and touch. All he knew was that it was cold, bitter cold, and he was tumbling, falling endlessly. He was alone, he was dying, he was . . . Frank Kinsey screamed as he was pulled through the shimmering surface. He didn't mean to. He couldn't help it.

Thinking back on it later, he decided that if he couldn't hear himself scream, no one else could either.

It sounded good, anyway.

He had no idea how long he fell. After a while it reminded him of a cartoon a colleague had had posted on her computer: three men falling, screaming, labeled "Bottomless Pit." The second panel, labeled "Twenty Years Later," was the same three men, still falling. But now they were casually examining their fingernails, kicking back on nothingness.

He was reasonably sure it wasn't actually twenty years before he fell out of cold eternity and into somewhere else, and he knew for certain he hadn't gotten blasé about it.

He was thumping and rolling across some very, very hard ground, completely disoriented and out of breath. He was no longer in an artificially illuminated cave in the guts of Cheyenne Mountain, Colorado; he was outside, under bright sunlight, and definitely somewhere else.

"What the hell—" he began as soon as he could get words out. But as he picked himself up he saw O'Neill and Carter already on their feet, Jackson stepping away from a Stargate identical to the one in Cheyenne Mountain, and Teal'C leaping gracefully out of the blue energy field, not one whit fazed by the experience. Almost immediately afterward came the transport, following Teal'C like a large mechanical puppy.

"Where—" he said before he could stop himself, and then he did stop, open-mouthed. No matter where—it wasn't Earth. It couldn't be.

The air smelled funny. Like pecans and walnuts and Brazil nuts. He had the sensation he was looking through rose-colored lenses; everything seemed to be tinted pink.

He felt groggy, heavier somehow.

There were three moons in the sunlit sky.

At first it didn't register; he saw three roundish pockmarked circles up above him and didn't know what they were. Then he looked at them again, his head snapping around so hard he almost gave himself whiplash. Those were moons. Moons. Three of them. *Three.* In shades of pink, from deep rose to delicate pearl. And it was daytime.

The last time he'd seen three moons in a single sky, George Lucas was responsible. But this was not a movie theater, or if it was, someone forgot to clean up all the rocks he'd bounced over.

And they were huge, too. The darkest one took up a good sixteenth of the sky and seemed almost within arm's reach. He reached up to try to touch it and staggered, losing his balance and falling in a heap.

"You cannot touch the satellite," Teal'C informed him gravely.

"I thought it was a moon," he sputtered.

"It is," Jackson responded. Jackson was checking over the gear draped all over the mechanical puppy. The others had barely given the sky a glance, and were paying no attention at all to the wonder overhead.

For the first time, it really sank in. He'd been awake all night thinking about it, but never really believing it in his bones until this moment: He was somewhere *else.* Somewhere with three moons, a place that smelled like a Planter's processing plant.

"As I said," Teal'C added. His characteristic frown deepened minutely. "You should get up."

Teal'C specialized in unnecessary advice, Kinsey

decided. He got up again, trying to get used to weighing about thirty-five pounds more than he did five minutes ago.

"Wow." It was a totally inadequate remark, but he felt he had to say *something*. "One giant step" had already been taken. Besides, it was more like one giant thud in this case. He rotated one arm experimentally, making sure it was still in its socket.

A roar like thunder echoed to the—west? Instantly, the team was on the alert, scanning the horizon.

"What was that?"

But O'Neill was waving them over to a small copse nearby and didn't look like he was ready to act as a tour guide. The other three team members took off at a businesslike jog, the cart trundling behind, and Kinsey had to scramble to keep up.

"What *was* that?" he repeated as they ducked into cover.

He could have sworn that Carter glared at him. O'Neill made an abrupt downward motion with his hand, and Kinsey opened his mouth again, determined to get an answer.

"Shut up," Jackson whispered harshly. "That was weapons fire."

Well, at least he had an answer. He looked around at the—no, they weren't really trees; they were more like upright vines, with tendrils snaking out to each other for support. Wherever light hit the vine, it pulsed outward like a beating heart, broadening its absorbent surface area. Distracted, he held one hand over one of the broad areas and watched fascinated as it shrank in the shadow.

The thunder rumbled again, and he looked up to see O'Neill studying him. The colonel looked as if he was beginning to regret the whole idea of bringing Kinsey along.

His next words supported that perception.

"Carter, I want you to go back to the Gate and shove our friend here back home," he said.

"Yes sir." The blonde major responded promptly and without the least sign of reluctance. Kinsey could have sworn that if anything, she was happy about the order.

"Wait! You can't. I haven't, haven't seen anything yet. I mean, where's the fire, Colonel? Where's the crowded room?" He was babbling, wild to stay. There were *aliens* out there, and he wanted to see!

O'Neill wasn't impressed, and Carter was on her feet, waiting, rifle in hand.

"All you've done so far is show me that we've got space travel. I thought you were trying to keep my mouth shut about it. Besides, I've been under fire before. I won't get in your way."

"Uh, Jack—" Jackson interrupted, at almost the same instant that Teal'C said sharply, "O'Neill!"

Kinsey turned to see what the other two were looking at and nearly choked. Standing in the little plain that separated their copse of vine-trees from the round Gate stood . . . something.

Aliens he wanted; aliens he got.

"Hasn't anybody told this world about the inverse square law?" O'Neill inquired plaintively.

The thing's body stood about twelve feet tall at what Kinsey couldn't help but identify as a shoulder, with a shiny black carapace and a triangular head that looked like nothing so much as a praying mantis. It balanced on six impossibly slender legs. Its body was almost a perfect cylinder, with a long, flexible tube at one end that terminated in the triangular head. The smooth hardness of its carapace blended into a wrinkled, leathery skin on the neck. If the alien stuck its head straight up in the air—which it didn't do often, preferring to keep it slightly above body height—the neck added another six feet of height.

In its arms it cradled something that was probably

a weapon. It too was long and roughly cylindrical, catching the sunlight as metal did. It reminded him of nothing so much as the rifle that Carter, beside him, carried at the ready. It was slung onto a harness woven around the thing's legs and body, not quite clothing but definitely manufactured.

Three more, similarly attired and armed, entered the clearing behind it. The tubular necks were snaking in all directions, wrapping around each other briefly as if in greeting and then twisting to scan the horizon. Two of the things stalked over to the Gate, examining it and the DHD as if they had never seen it before, sticking necks through and curving them around to look at themselves as if locking their necks through a hoop.

"Uh, sir—" Carter said hesitantly.

"Belay that order. Dammit," O'Neill directed, and sighed. Without taking his eyes off the aliens, he went on, "Okay, Kinsey, you wanted space travel and alien worlds, you got it. Let's see what you think the man on the street on Earth ought to know about it.

"Dave Morley didn't say anything about tubenecks on P7X-924. He was supposed to rescue one of our teams on this world from the Goa'uld. Teal'C, what are *those* things?"

"Those aren't Gold?"

"Goa'uld," Jackson corrected. "There's a glottal stop in the middle of the word." The younger man was staring intently through the camcorder as it ran quietly, taking data.

"Not the time for a linguistics lesson, Daniel. Teal'C?"

"I do not know," the answer came. "I have never seen these people before, and I have never heard them described. They appear to have been attracted by the activation of the Gate."

"I agree, and I don't like it," O'Neill muttered.

"They don't seem to be familiar with the Gate," Daniel remarked, still filming. "And that pattern of digitation—I wonder if they're from here at all. Maybe they got here in ships." He kept on talking softly, providing a running commentary for the film. "That neck-twining thing looks like a giraffe mating dance. Appears to be related to communication, although these people do vocalize."

People? Kinsey wondered, unable to tear his eyes away from the creatures now directly between the little party of humans and their only means of escape. The creatures were making a chirruping sound as they spread out in the fashion of recon teams from time immemorial. Both Jackson and Carter were running their camcorders. Kinsey's hands itched for a camera.

"They look like something out of a Heinlein novel," Carter remarked as she changed out tapes. "*Starship Troopers,* maybe. Or *Tunnel in the Sky.*"

"Yeah, well, the good guys always won in his books, but we don't have any such guarantees." O'Neill was on one knee, his rifle rested butt-down on the ground, shielding himself behind a low-hanging vine. "I wonder if this is what Dave really saw. If it is, then they're responsible for his breakdown, too, which means we probably don't want to walk up and introduce ourselves. What we're gonna do is sneak the hell around them and try to get to the city again and see if we can figure out what happened."

"There are cities, too?" Kinsey said, unable to keep the rapture out of his voice.

O'Neill glared at him. "Your job is to keep out of our way and to stay alive, in that order, Kinsey. I'm not going to lose one of my people because of a *journalist.* Understand?"

"I've been in combat," the journalist retorted with an injured look. "I know the drill."

"I've got news for you, mister. Out here there

aren't any drills, because it's different every time. We owe you nothing, you understand? But if I give you an order you're going to follow it, right now, no questions. Got that?" O'Neill's voice was low, his words rapid-fire.

All four of them were looking at him now, their faces expressionless. *This is a team,* Kinsey realized, a real team, *not just four people thrown together for an assignment.* He had seen this before in tightly bonded military units, and he knew O'Neill meant exactly what he said. His own life was his responsibility. They took care of each other first.

From the clearing behind them came a gentle hissing sound from the triangular heads. It sent a cold chill down his back. Kinsey swallowed twice. "I got it."

The hissing sound increased exponentially, and SG-1 and their unwanted guest snapped their attention back to the clearing, flattening themselves even closer to the ground. The tubenecks were becoming agitated, their triangular heads swinging back and forth.

"They're looking for something," Carter whispered.

"And I think they found it," O'Neill responded in a low voice. "Seven o'clock."

Kinsey traced the imaginary line. The four tubenecks had converged in front of the Gate, their necks twisting together like courting giraffes. A flickering speck at seven o'clock was rapidly becoming larger.

The speck became a dot, a blotch against the sky, splitting and coming together again.

"It's a moth!" Carter sputtered. "A giant moth!"

And it was: a giant moth with extra legs—arms?—folded up close to its thorax. Unlike the tubenecks, it didn't seem to be carrying anything. Its wingspan stretched at least fifteen feet across, in three sections, the largest on top, a smaller wing segment in the middle, with the third segment midway between the other two in size. It was brown, with white and black markings scattered randomly across its entire surface. Its body, from one end to the other, was longer than a tall man. It didn't have antennae.

And its thorax was sheathed in something that didn't look like moth fur.

"Oh, come on. Those things aren't Godzilla. That *can't* be Mothra."

"Could it just be an animal?" Carter asked.

"I don't know," Jackson responded. "It's tough to tell yet whether it has intelligence or not. It seems to recognize the tubenecks, though. It's obviously perceived them and is responding to their presence. From the reaction of the tubenecks it's an aggressive move."

"Scientists," O'Neill muttered.

Teal'C was ignoring this byplay, Kinsey noted. It appeared to be an excellent example to follow.

Both camcorders whirred steadily.

The tubenecks split apart, scattering to four quarters, and the moth hovered between and above them. Even at this distance they could hear the beating of its brown wings against the air, see a shimmer as some kind of dust fell from the wings to the ground.

Then the tubenecks fired their weapons simultaneously, with a stream of blue fire. The brown wings burst into flame and the moth fell, screaming thinly. The tubenecks converged on it.

"I can't see what they're doing," Daniel Jackson fretted, standing up to get a better view for his camera.

"I don't care what they're doing. This is a really good time to retreat," O'Neill retorted. "Let's go, people."

CHAPTER THIRTEEN

They crept through the underbrush, pausing only to disentangle themselves from the vines and creepers. Kinsey found himself panting to keep up with the others as they made their way around a small outcrop of rock and slithered to the top to study their back trail. The tubenecks were heading in the opposite direction, and all five breathed a sigh of relief.

Kinsey took the opportunity to look around. One of the three moons was setting, huge against the horizon; a thin trail of smoke twisting up from the ground marred its red-gold beauty. Eastward of the smoke, jagged reddish-purple mountains defined the distance. Patches of trees—or what passed for trees—dotted the plains below them. In the middle distance he could see the Gate, rising out of the ground as the only object that was clearly artifact, manufactured by intelligent hands. Or handlike objects. *Would that be handibles? Handoids?* Not far away, the ruined body of the moth still smoldered.

He glanced around at the others, who were taking a break after making sure there was no immediate threat. "Wow," he said.

Carter looked up at him and gave him a brief grin. "Yeah, wow."

At least somebody appreciated the sheer wonder of the situation. He was beginning to think that the three men on the team were either entirely without imagination or simply jaded by too much exposure to the unearthly.

O'Neill was watching him too, his face expressionless. There was no telling what kind of thoughts were moving behind those dark eyes.

"Colonel," Kinsey said, trying to be conciliatory, "I really *don't* want to get in the way. I especially don't want to get myself or anyone else killed. So do you think you could just fill me in on the basics, so I have some clue?"

O'Neill's lips tightened. Before he could say anything, Jackson spoke up. "He's right, Jack. He's here; time to give him Briefing B."

"Yeah. Like, who are these Goa'gurgle you've mentioned?"

O'Neill waved a hand to Jackson, who took it as permission and assumed his lecturing-professor persona.

"The Goa'uld are intelligent aliens, with space-travel capability. We think they found the Stargate system rather than built it themselves, but they've found it very convenient, probably because it's faster than ship travel. We're not certain where their original homeworld is. In their natural state they look sort of like worms, or lampreys, as adults, but before that they spend several years in a larval form. In order to survive as larvae, they have to achieve a symbiotic relationship with another species. They first visited Earth at least three millennia ago, with the intention of harvesting human beings for use as hosts."

Kinsey found his mouth open, an *oh come on now* hovering unspoken. Then he glanced up at the sky again, remembering the tubenecks and the moths and the conflict he had just witnessed, and decided to let Jackson continue uninterrupted.

"A few decades ago we discovered the Stargate on Earth. More recently we found out how to operate it." Jackson paused and bit his lip, obviously trying to decide what parts of a very large and complex story to tell. The other members of the team remained silent, listening. "Anyway, the first world we found was the planet Abydos. Abydos turned out to be one of many planets the Goa'uld had seeded with human beings from various cultures and periods of Earth history. It also provided the clues we needed to operate the Gate to reach those other planets. This is one of those planets."

"Ra," O'Neill said laconically.

"I was trying to be brief," Jackson responded.

O'Neill shrugged.

"Who's Ra?" Kinsey said predictably. None of this had been in the manual he'd read the night before.

"Ra was a Goa'uld who was using the people of Abydos as fodder—harvesting them as hosts." Jackson's voice was suddenly tight and uneven, as if this part of the narrative had personal meaning for him. "We—well, Jack—destroyed him.

"We thought that was the end of it, but another Goa'uld discovered the coordinates for Earth. That brought Earth into direct conflict with the Goa'uld."

"Okay," Kinsey said, trying to buy time to choose the first of the dozens of questions that were vying for precedence. "So we're at war with these guys. They've actually launched an attack on Earth itself? Why the hell shouldn't the world know?"

"Because right now the Goa'uld aren't unified, any more than we are. But they're perfectly capable of taking advantage of a world split into factions pro-alien and con. Before that happens, we're trying to accumulate information about them, their various factions, plus all the other worlds out here. Apophis, the one we've got really ticked off at us, apparently doesn't have all the resources he needs to launch an overwhelming attack right now. We're buying time, and we've got no guarantees we're going to win," O'Neill said wearily. "It's bad enough that we can't even get support from our own government. What makes you think the whole world will cooperate?"

"I take it you're referring to my father."

O'Neill tilted a half-nod of agreement. "He thinks we can win because God is on our side. At the same time he's scared to death we're going to bring something back through the Gate that'll destroy us all. He's already tried to shut us down once. The fact that it wouldn't stop Apophis doesn't seem to matter to him."

"Consistency was never one of my father's biggest virtues." Kinsey considered. It had been a long time since he'd agreed with his father on much of anything. "So you're saying he arranged to have me come out here to blow the whistle on you in the hope that world pressure will succeed where he failed?"

"Give the man a cigar," O'Neill said wryly.

"So why am I *here*?" Here, on an alien world, weighing more than he ought to, breathing funny-tasting air, watching aliens go at each other like something from *Dinosaurus* . . .

"Because General Hammond said so. I guess he thinks you have something your father hasn't got."

"Common sense, maybe," Jackson offered. He slapped hard at an insect that had lighted on his arm. "Ouch."

"Or maybe sending me to another world is just the biggest bribe that's ever been offered a newspaperman in the history of the Earth."

"That too," O'Neill agreed. "We're hoping you'll stay bought."

He grinned despite himself. "So what's the deal on this world?" It was easier to breathe now, Kinsey found. His body was slowly adjusting to the heavier gravity. "What's happening here?" His briefing manuals had contained nothing about where the Gates led, or aliens. Or Goa'uld.

Carter, who was unloading the mechanical puppy, took up the story. Kinsey was fascinated at the volume and variety of materiel that piled up beside the metal cart. Weapons—some of which he identified as such by default, having never seen them before—supplies, explosives. Carter passed around packs as she talked, and the others busily loaded up.

"This is the world we designated P7X-924. Our team, SG-1, made first contact here a couple of months ago. We found a human colony that has been here, as far as we can tell, for several hundred years; the origin seems to be East Africa. They're a peaceful trading and farming community, pre-industrial, with a good understanding of at least this part of this planet's ecosystem. Our mission is to find allies, tools, technology, anything that Earth can use against the Goa'uld, and if there's a cure for cancer lying around we'll get that too."

"And if you find something the U.S. could use against, say, China?"

"We've got our mission," O'Neill said firmly. He didn't look at all uncomfortable. "Policy isn't our bailiwick."

"Besides," Jackson put in, "the human communities we've found have all been far less technologically advanced than Earth is. And we've got bigger worries than China out here."

O'Neill shot the blond man a bland look and continued.

"Anyway. The Etaans have adapted some of the local vegetation and come up with what might be some new antibiotics. So we sent SG-4, a research team, in to do a baseline study.

"Things went bad. A couple of members of SG-4 made it back to tell us that most of the team was dead but some had been taken prisoner. David Morley was supposed to launch a retrieval operation. You saw how well that worked out when you were in the infirmary. We're here to figure out what the hell happened."

"So the ones who came through when Morley had me—"

"Nope, that was SG-9 on a different mission entirely. They were doing a combat reconnaissance on a totally different world. It's not just the four of us, you know. There are several operations going at once at all times."

The colonel fell silent, and Kinsey tried to sort through all the information about SGs, planets, Goa'uld. He wished he had a camcorder of his own, or at least a pencil and a piece of paper. It was too much.

And not enough.

"So what are *those* things?" Kinsey asked, jerking a thumb back toward the now-deserted plain marked only by the Stargate.

"Damned if I know," O'Neill shrugged.

Kinsey decided there was something seriously warped about O'Neill's sense of humor. And he liked it.

The little outcrop of rocks was developing all the signs of becoming a very comfortable base camp. Carter was busy filling four sets of backpacks as they talked.

"So what do you think happened to the people— the humans, from Earth, I mean—who live here?"

"They've probably been taken by Goa'uld troops to be hosts." There was a strained harshness to Jackson's answer. There was definitely something going on there, something personal. Kinsey made a mental note to follow up on it sometime. Maybe he could buy the man a drink. He didn't look like a straight-arrow military type.

"When you say hosts—what exactly do you mean?"

He noted with some interest that three of them glanced simultaneously at Teal'C before Jackson said evenly, "The Goa'uld are a parasitic race. They need other species to live with. In larval form it's a symbiotic relationship. When they become adults they take a new host and—it's not symbiotic any more. They take over."

"So they look human? Or—I guess the hosts are, but can you see the aliens too? At the same time?"

"No. Not exactly."

"So how do you know whether you're dealing with a real human or a pod person?"

"You'll know," Jackson said dryly. "The behavior differences are—explicit."

"Okay, now that we have the exposition over with, can we get on with the mission?" O'Neill snapped.

"But—" Kinsey started to say that he had more questions, many, many more questions, but the expression on the colonel's face persuaded him that perhaps this wasn't a good time. He swallowed his curiosity and nodded.

"Okay, let's move out." All the packs were filled. Carter handed one to Kinsey as well, an odd flat rectangle, and he grunted as he slung it across his shoulders. He thought he was in shape, but he was glad he hadn't bragged about it.

He was even gladder when he realized that the pack was just as affected by the heavier gravity as he himself was, and none of the others made an issue of it. Everything had been divided up evenly, too, he noticed, so he was carrying as much weight as Carter and O'Neill and Jackson and Teal'C were. They seemed to concentrate on firepower; he had no idea what was in the rectangle.

Teal'C. What a weird name. Neither he nor Jackson wore any rank insignia, unless that funny tattoo on the black man's forehead counted. Kinsey tucked that thought, too, away for greater consideration later.

The five of them slipped and slid down the little outcrop and headed across the plain at a fast trot, keeping to the shelter of the vegetation, heading for the thin line of smoke. The dark-red moon it marred had set, but the other two between them shed as much light as—a sun? What was the sun of this world, he wondered. A red giant? How far from it did this world revolve?

Were there other worlds in this system? Worlds with living beings? Could they visit them, too?

He barely noticed when the smell of nuts was replaced with something else less palatable. He was puffing as they came through a thin line of "trees," and so nearly ran up Teal'C's back when the big man stopped abruptly.

"Down!" O'Neill whispered, and Kinsey was never so grateful to obey an order in his life. He pressed his face into something that looked remarkably like grass, breathing hard.

"Quiet!"

That particular order wasn't quite as easy to obey, but he tried, opening his jaws wide so his breath didn't whistle quite so much, controlling the heaving of his lungs as best he could.

"Wha—?"

He lifted his head at last to see his companions arrayed in a skirmish line on either side of him, peering through the blades.

Holy sh—

He couldn't even finish the expletive. He had never seen anything like the scene that unrolled down the gentle slope in front of him.

He had been present at the uncovering of mass graves in Kosovo. He'd seen the rubble of downtown Sarajevo, the damage that SCUD missiles inflicted on Baghdad.

He had never seen anything like this. Surely no American reporter had seen anything like this since—since Gettysburg, maybe.

Carter, sprawled on the ground to his left, was pale but watchful. Teal'C, to his right, had permitted two deep lines to mar his forehead. He couldn't see Jackson and O'Neill, lying on Teal'C's far side.

They couldn't see very much. The ground didn't conveniently slope away as it had from their last vantage point, so their angle of vision was restricted. It was a blessing, Kinsey thought. It was a wide expanse of mostly open space; on the other side he could see low hills. At their base was something that looked like structures, irregular but unnatural. Whatever they were blended into the hills behind them; they'd be barely noticeable if they weren't yet another source of the smoke disfiguring the sky.

Closer to, the ground before them smoked and bubbled like a gigantic, overheated marsh. Stalking not six feet in front of the frozen humans was one of the tubenecks, making a keening sound and dragging two of its legs and half its cylindrical body behind it. The other half was simply missing. Blue-green ooze bled from the hole where the creature's side and back had been, and things were falling out of it, internal organs and systems. Like the ground it dragged itself over, the remains of the tubeneck's body were smoking and bubbling, its shiny black carapace expanding like heated plastic.

The alien paused, its triangular head swinging back and forth to survey the humans lying prone before it, its horizontal jaws working, and then it toppled ungracefully, twitched, and lay still.

Beyond the dead alien lay dozens—hundreds—more of its kind, in various stages of meltdown. And the tubenecks weren't alone; there were some other things scattered among them too, things that might have had wings and certainly had claws—the moth creatures.

The devastation covered acres. It was a soup of dead things, interrupted only by tree trunks sticking up nakedly like exclamation points. Kinsey looked for, but did not find, signs of human death. There were no bloated bodies, no staring single-faceted eyes or gaping jaws.

Oddly, there also wasn't much smell. What there was, was distinctly unpleasant, but a scene like this on Earth would have reeked for miles, and they hadn't even noticed the aroma before nearly stumbling on the battlefield.

O'Neill made a signal, and the team started wriggling backward into the shelter of the trees. Carter pulled Kinsey along with them, grabbing his shoulder when he didn't respond fast enough.

When they got to their feet they could see the extent of the damage even more clearly and could hear the sounds the dying aliens made. The wind shifted, bringing a concentrated whiff of what odor there was, and all five of them gagged simultaneously.

Kinsey decided this was no time to ask questions. He stood silent, breathing shallowly through his mouth and trying not to taste the air, while O'Neill consulted with his team.

"I don't think we're gonna cross that area," the colonel said at last. "I really don't like the way that ground looks. Let's take the long way around and hope that whatever it is, is over."

"Second that, sir," Carter said with feeling. Teal'C and Jackson nodded soberly.

"Teal'C, do you have any idea—"

The big man shook his head.

"What about the weapons? Recognize any of them?"

Teal'C shook his head again. "We found signs of what could have been such battles, from time to time," he said, shifting his pack into place. "But we never remained long, and never saw what caused such devastation."

"It looked almost as if that alien had been sprayed with something." Jackson commented.

"Super insect spray?"

The look the archaeologist gave the colonel should have quelled him. It wasn't enough, of course, to quell Jack O'Neill. "Well, they look like bugs," he said with mock defensiveness. Then, more seriously, "It did look like a spray. I didn't see any holes that would be made by projectile wounds." He looked to Carter for confirmation, and she shook her head.

How could they have maintained the presence of mind to assess the kind of damage the alien had undergone? Kinsey wondered. How could they stand around discussing it so calmly?

"All right. The last time we were here we saw a trail over the hill, remember? We'll try that route and see what we can see. The bear went over the mountain—"

"Please, O'Neill, do not sing," Teal'C said seriously. Carter smothered a grin.

Kinsey was still in shock, trying to assimilate. The others might take this kind of thing for granted, might even make jokes, but this wasn't the way he'd planned to spend the afternoon.

And there was more. They asked Teal'C for his opinion of the aliens and their weapons as if he was in a position to know a lot more about it than they were. What was it he'd said? *We found signs of what could have been such battles, from time to time. But we never remained long, and never saw what caused such devastation.* Who was the "we" to whom the big man referred? Obviously he was more widely traveled than the other members of the team, but even he had never encountered tubenecks before.

Kinsey realized with a shock that he was beginning to take travel between worlds for granted too. When confronted with multilegged intelligent alien life-forms busy trying to exterminate each other, a little detail like a chilly wormhole was barely worth noticing.

They backed away from the scene of the battle, keeping to the trees, moving at right angles to the smoke. That smoke was suddenly considerably more ominous than it had been a half an hour before.

CHAPTER FOURTEEN

The circuitous route around the killing field seemed to take forever. Every time they thought they'd passed it they saw more evidence of battle. Even where the vegetation was still a more or less healthy pink, it was dry and crunched beneath their boots.

O'Neill called for rest breaks three times, the third time—finally away from the pervasive, if discreet, smell of death—breaking out field rations. Kinsey found a packet of nuts in his MRE, looked at it thoughtfully, and decided he wasn't very fond of cashews after all. The others didn't eat theirs either, he noticed.

Daniel Jackson sat with his arms on his updrawn knees, staring at nothing in particular as he swigged water from his canteen. Kinsey sat beside him and rubbed his legs, trying to ease the cramping from the unaccustomed exercise.

"I take it you're not military," Kinsey said, attempting to strike up a friendly conversation about something, anything other than what they had just seen.

Jackson gave him a considering look, not as suspicious as O'Neill's but not particularly forthcoming either. "No, I'm not." A winged insect, or this world's equivalent, buzzed by, and Jackson took a halfhearted swipe at it, nearly knocking his glasses off in the process. The insect went spinning, and

Jackson winced as a bubble of bright-red blood squeezed from his thumb. "Ow. That's some set of claws on that sucker."

"You're an anthropologist, right?"

"Archaeologist, actually." The bug came back, and Jackson swatted at it again. Kinsey wondered if the blond man welcomed the distraction. It landed beside the scientist, and he studied it as if there were nothing more fascinating in the whole world.

"So how did you get involved in this whole thing?" He could feel the eyes of the other team members boring into him, but this was his job, after all. Besides, he was genuinely curious.

"I help translate." Clearly Jackson wasn't interested in giving out his life story, but even he could hear the abruptness in his response. In a more conciliatory tone he went on, "My background's in ancient Middle Eastern cultures, and that turned out to be one of the hot spots of Goa'uld visitation."

"So those things back there aren't Goa'uld?" Kinsey made a genuine effort to pronounce the word correctly. He was rewarded with a brief smile. The man must have been devastating as a graduate assistant. He didn't look much older than graduate assistants Kinsey had seen; late twenties, very early thirties, tops, and he wouldn't look that old if it weren't for the sense of wariness in otherwise guileless blue eyes. He had the look of a man who'd been bitten by the universe a few times, but hadn't quite reached the stage of cynicism about it that O'Neill had. A dreamer, Kinsey decided. A dreamer of the day, one of the dangerous ones who had the capability and determination to make his dreams real.

"Oh no," Jackson said. "'We don't have any idea what those are. Every time we go through the Gate, we find something new. It's a big universe."

"So you've gone through the Gate a lot?" The question was a little too disingenuous, and he decided to be blunt. "How long have you been using this Stargate of yours?"

Jackson was silent for a moment, thinking, maybe weighing alternative answers. "Years," he said at last. "Mostly the last couple of years. We didn't know how to get anywhere, how to use the Gate for a long time. Abydos was—" he took a deep breath and let it out. "Abydos was an accident. The Gate was pre-set for that location."

"How many locations are there?"

Jackson shrugged. "Hundreds. Thousands. We don't really know."

"And do you find new alien races every time?" He couldn't believe he was asking these questions, seriously asking and getting serious answers back. And for the life of him he couldn't think of a lead for the story anymore. Usually by this time he had the first half of his story, or at least the first story in the series, mapped out. Not this time.

"No. The coordinates we have are for Goa'uld worlds, so mostly we find humans. Sometimes Goa'uld. Sometimes Jaffa."

"What are 'Jaffa'?"

"My people," Teal'C interjected. "Slaves to the Goa'uld. Hosts to their larvae. Their warriors."

Kinsey twisted around to face him. Teal'C's customary expression looked very much like one of those statues on Easter Island, he thought, only much rounder. The deep frown was the same, though. "You're a Jaffa?" the word was unfamiliar in his mouth.

"Yes. I have renounced my allegiance to the Goa'uld."

"Uh, don't take this wrong, please but . . . does that mean you're not human? From Earth?"

Teal'C nodded sharply, apparently unconcerned. "That is correct."

"Oh." Once when he was a little kid, he'd dumped

out a bowl full of goldfish onto the kitchen floor. For the first time he felt he understood how the goldfish felt as their mouths opened and closed uselessly. He couldn't stop staring at the man. Except that, apparently, he wasn't, strictly speaking, a *man*.

He *looked* human. Except of course for that symbol on his forehead, which looked like a gilded scar. The guy had one head, two arms, two legs, hands that strongly resembled George Foreman's. In his set of regular jungle cammie fatigues, he would blend in with any American military unit.

Alien? Couldn't be. They had to be making fun of him, seeing just how credulous the reporter would be in his search for a story. *Aliens looking exactly like Earth humans are living among us!*

He *still* didn't really believe it, he realized. Part of him still thought he was sitting in the briefing room at the Visitors Center for the Cheyenne Mountain Complex, listening to Captain Weikman go on and on about tracking Santa Claus from the North Pole on December 24, the primary role these days of Air Force Space Defense Systems.

And the team members were watching him again, waiting to see how he would react. He experienced a slow burn of resentment that they could sit there chewing mystery meat and take all this for granted, that they could believe this, live this every day. Didn't they appreciate the wonder and the scope of what they were doing?

For the first time he asked himself, quite seriously, *What the hell am I doing here?* It wasn't a question about what *he* was doing, so much as it was why he was here with these people who didn't respect him or his work, were cooperating with obvious reluctance, and had no intention of ever letting him use the information they provided him. He was being shown a banquet and told he would never, ever be able to eat it. And these people could feast on it every day and considered it no more than another course of MREs.

"Okay, folks, let's hit the road," O'Neill said. "We've got places to go and people to see."

Maybe one's sense of wonder got burned out when you went to new worlds every week, Kinsey thought. Or maybe, he reminded himself sternly, the immediate possibility of getting oneself killed tended to shut down the *ooooh-ahhhh* reflex. He took himself by the mental scruff of the neck and shook himself sternly. Resentment? It was jealousy, pure and simple. These people—this unit, anyway, given that they weren't all quite *people*—got to do things he'd only fantasized about. He'd always wanted to visit Barsoom, and now here he was, with a bunch of people who were incredibly blasé about it all. It made him feel like a tourist, like a kid at a science fiction convention instead of a seasoned, experienced professional. Well, he could be just as matter-of-fact about strange new worlds and alien sidekicks as the next guy. So *there*.

He tucked the debris of his meal back into his pack and staggered to his feet to join the rest of them. Okay, so not all outer space creatures were bug-eyed monsters. At least *some* of them were. He could accept that. He hoped.

On the other hand—he chuckled suddenly. The image that had just popped into his head was priceless.

"What's funny?" Carter asked, keeping pace beside him. At least she was human. If it turned out that she wasn't, Kinsey decided he didn't want to know. Some things were just too horrible to contemplate.

"I'm just imagining what the look on my father's face must have been when *he* first heard all this," Kinsey sputtered. "I wish I'd been there to see it. He must have had a fit."

"Just about," the blonde officer said cheerfully. "Has he always had this denial problem?"

"Always." With his determined change in mood, he allowed himself to realize that the major was really very attractive. Or maybe it was just the automatic rifle slung over her shoulder in such a businesslike fashion. He found himself wondering if she was married. "How'd *you* get hauled into this?"

"Oh, I volunteered." Once again that impish grin, and then she lengthened her stride and passed him, easily catching up with the three other members of the team ahead of him.

It seemed to take most of the afternoon to circle the battle plain and reach the hills and the signs of construction at their base.

Wonder what's gonna pop out at us this time, he thought. He was almost looking forward to it.

Jack O'Neill allowed part of his mind—the really irritated part—to keep track of their unwanted guest, while the majority of his thoughts were focused on what lay ahead. On their first visit to P7X-924, he'd been impressed by the warmth, friendliness, and practical intelligence of the human population of the place. The suggestion that the Goa'uld had found them again after centuries was deeply disturbing. The evidence of battle behind them was even worse.

It was a big galaxy out there. Weren't the Goa'uld bad enough? Were they going to have to battle tubenecks too?

He made a mental note to ask the Nox about this if he ever had the chance. He hadn't had a chance to look at the tubenecks' opponents close up, though he had an impression of mothlike wings and very businesslike claws. As an older, wiser, and infinitely more tolerant race than Earth had yet produced, the Nox were sometimes willing to share information with their upstart neighbors. He wondered what Kinsey would make of the Nox sky city. Not that he'd ever managed to visit it himself, of course—the people of Earth were considered a bad influence on the impressionable young—but still, it was pretty amazing even from a distance.

Then there was Morley. Nothing in Morley's report had hinted at two new alien races, apparently at war with each other. If O'Neill hadn't verified the coordinates himself he'd be wondering if they'd arrived at the right planet. *Oops, sorry, wrong address, we meant to deliver the nukes next door.* But Morley had gone well and truly off the deep end. Could it have been the tubenecks and the whatevers that did for him? Did he ascribe his casualties to the Goa'uld because that was what he could cope with?

Did it really matter?

Of course it mattered. Three Stargate teams had come to this world, and two of them had come back in tatters. He felt responsible. They'd come to this world expecting no trouble at all, based on the word of one Jack O'Neill, Colonel, USAF. They had a right to think this assignment would be interesting—problematic maybe, but mostly safe. What had gone wrong?

"For crying out loud, Jack, are you in a race?"

He glanced over to see Daniel puffing beside him, stretching his legs to keep up. Over his shoulder he spotted Kinsey, a good twenty yards back, gamely struggling.

"Okay, okay." He stopped and waited impatiently for everyone to catch up. It wasn't his fault he had long legs. Now that he was stopped, though, he could feel his own lungs heaving the heavy air in and out, feel his own heart beating hard. He needed to slow down and take it easy. Easier, anyway. No point in wearing yourself out right before a firefight.

Was he expecting a firefight?

Yes, he was, and looking forward to it, too. He'd

liked the Etaans. He wanted to find out who these new critters were and kick their butts. Hard.

Kinsey tripped as he covered the last few yards, and O'Neill closed his eyes in pain. Hammond must have been out of his mind to send this jerk along. This wasn't supposed to be a guided tour or a babysitting expedition. They had work to do, dammit.

To his credit, Kinsey got up reasonably quickly and uttered no complaint. He was grateful for the unscheduled stop, it was obvious; he leaned over and clutched his knees, gulping air. But the others were breathing hard too, and they were in fighting trim. O'Neil wondered what constituted "fighting trim" for a journalist. Fully armed with sharpened pencils, maybe?

At the least the guy had the sense to laugh about his father. That was a *big* point in his favor.

"Okay, the city is just past this last line of trees," he said as the team gathered around. "According to Dave Morley, they were suckered in. So we're going to take it slow and easy and keep our eyes peeled, not just for Jaffa but for our other unidentified friends as well."

Because the inhabitants called the little town with the twin towers Etaa, that worked for the name of the world too, SG-1 had decided. One of the interesting problems SG-4 had set itself was to discover from just which area of Earth the ancestors of the Etaans had been kidnapped. Some of the other worlds, such as Simarka—designated P3X-593 in the arcane numbering system used by SGC—had very clear roots in specific Earth cultures. Simarka's inhabitants were descended from Mongolian herders and horsemen. The Cimmerians came from northern Europe. The Byrsa on P3X-1279 were an eclectic mix of Greek, Celtic, and Germanic. Etaa had the same fascinating combination of many cultures, in this case with hints of Syrian, early Byzantine, and more than just a touch of Masai. Their economy was based on trade and cattle, with some mining; they had really elaborate gold jewelry, necklaces and earrings and bracelets that would have been hot items on Earth. But SG-1 wasn't in the business of setting up trading partnerships, and that had almost undone them until they realized the rules of this new culture. *Everything* on Etaa was a matter of trade.

The Etaans were very tall, very black, very dignified. O'Neill had had a crick in his neck for a week after finishing the preliminary talks with Shostoka'an, the principal leader. He still thought it wasn't quite fair that Shostoka'an's badge of office was a towering plume of almost-ostrich feathers; the woman was already nearly eight feet tall. He rubbed at his neck, remembering. He had liked Shostoka'an a lot. He wondered what had happened to her.

Daniel reached down and picked a candy wrapper out of some bruised vegetation, a look of disgust on his face. "This must be where Morley's men stopped," he said. "Litterbugs."

The team paused in the trees to survey the town.

Etaa was spread out along the base of the hills, a bubble of human habitation bounded by a tall—a *very* tall—vine-woven fence. Some of the vines were in flower, giving the city wall an incongruously festive appearance. Beyond the fence they could see a few widely spaced roofs, shaped like onion domes but fashioned of some kind of straw thatch bundles. The main gate in front of them, a double door of wide wood planks nailed together by crosspieces, was flanked by one and a half cylindrical stone towers. The intact one was about fifty feet tall, providing a vantage point not only for the surrounding countryside but for the interior of the town as well. The other tower looked as if something had hit it with terrific force, knocking the top off at an angle and blasted to pieces. The gate between them sagged, all of its supports on one side vanished. There were several windows in the tower, higher than a Western Earth eye would look for them, and they made jagged dark holes in the ruins.

"This is where they fired on the Jaffa," O'Neill mused out loud. "They took out that right-hand tower with a grenade launcher—lucky it didn't burn the whole place down. They reported the force field right in front of the main gate."

"It's still really quiet in there," Carter said, and shifted her weapon slightly. "There's something wrong. Unless it really is deserted, but that doesn't feel right."

"I agree." O'Neill continued to study the brown towers. There weren't any bird critters nesting on top of the flat platform at the top of the intact one—in fact, he couldn't hear much of anything at all. The tall wooden gates sagged open, the supports on the right side vanished along with most of the tower they'd been connected to. There was no flow of merchants passing in or out, no bargaining going on in the shade of a hide tent. Etaa was humbled, not a proud city any more but a little, primitive town that had fallen to a siege.

O'Neill looked at the trees around and behind them. There was no sign of return fire from the Jaffa; the vegetation looked healthy and untouched.

"O'Neill, look here." Teal'C had taken a flank position some hundred yards north, scouting the smaller city gate on that side. O'Neill signaled Carter and the albatross to stay in place, while he and Daniel faded back to cross over to Teal'C's position.

"Uh-oh," Daniel said, in a masterpiece of understatement.

Approximately a third of the north boundary wall of Etaa was slumped, as if subjected to months of heavy rain that had pounded its mud bricks back into liquid, its woven vines and log supports into a tangled mass. It still retained some form, though, creating a Dali-esque image of a wall. Half the gate had melted too, the wood planks flowing onto the ground as if spilled. He could see bubbles, but they didn't move; they were more like shells, as if the damage had been done long enough ago for the liquid to cool and solidify again. The remainder of the wall—and the gate—looked perfectly, obscenely normal. Whatever the weapon was, it could be targeted very precisely. Even if, in this case, it was the wrong target. He hoped it was.

"I think the attackers, whoever they may be, are gone," Teal'C said judiciously. "This does not appear to be the result of a direct assault on Etaa, but more likely collateral damage related to the battleground we passed earlier."

"I am *so* glad you think so," O'Neill remarked. Then, at Daniel's sharp look, he added defensively, "I am. Really!"

"Just checking," Daniel murmured.

"Well, I guess we'll have to do a little recce." O'Neill stepped out of the tree line long enough to circle his hand in the air and pump his fist twice, then faded back into cover to wait for Carter and their journalist to form up on his position. Frank Kinsey was certainly getting an eyeful on this trip, he thought. Talk about an exclusive.

A few minutes later the missing members of their group reappeared, looked at the ruined wall and winced. Even Kinsey, O'Neill noticed, seemed able to draw the proper conclusions, even though he had never even seen the residents of the town, much less sat down with the Etaa for a formal meal of blood and milk. Collateral damage or not, based on this it was likely that Shostoka'an and most of her people *were* dead.

"Teal'C, I want you and Daniel to stay here with Kinsey and keep an eye out. I don't want to get trapped the way Morley did. Carter, you come with me, and we'll see if we can find anybody alive in there." Anybody, in this case, definitely included the missing members of SG-4 and anyone Morley had left behind as well.

Surprisingly, Teal'C shook his head. "It would be a better use of our forces to continue reconnaissance around the perimeter."

O'Neill paused. Teal'C was right, but he wanted to keep Kinsey out of the way.

On the other hand, he didn't want Kinsey *in* the way, either, and cutting his mobility in half was definitely in that category.

"All right. Circle around, and we'll look for you here in two hours." With that, O'Neill and Carter took off for the melted wall, making use of every scrap of available cover. The others watched until they disappeared, and then went on their own assignment.

CHAPTER FIFTEEN

The buildings, streets, and open places of Etaa enclosed by its walls covered almost a square mile. When O'Neill and Carter picked their way through the solidified slush, they could see that whatever the weapon was that had destroyed the wall hadn't stopped there. Every formerly solid structure in line with the wall for at least a quarter mile showed signs of slumping and damage.

"That's some weapon," Carter remarked uneasily, poking at a bubble on the ground with the barrel of her rifle. The bubble cracked, releasing a weak puff of gas, and she backed away rapidly, weapon ready, even though there was nothing to fire at but rapidly dissipating pink gas. An insect flying by passed through the mist and promptly fell down dead.

"Uh, don't breathe that," O'Neill suggested.

"Roger that, sir." They stepped carefully around the bubbles and past the melted wall, stopping first to scan the area on the other side and, when no sign of life was detected, to examine the melted wall surface.

"What would do that, Major? High temps?"

Carter shook her head. "I'd expect ash and scorch marks," she said. "This looks like something chemical. I have no idea what, though." Removing a glass vial from her pack, she carefully chipped away a sample of the wall and tucked it away. "This stuff is really hard, too. Harder than I'd expect from adobe."

"Make sure you check that vial. Wouldn't want it melting through the container," O'Neill instructed. He couldn't control a frisson of nerves.

"Yes sir." Carter could have objected—it was an obvious precaution, after all—but she simply nodded and took the order as meant.

"Okay, let's go."

Their boots crunched on the melt surface, and by mutual consent they moved away from the path of the damage and onto the softer, if considerably less sterilized, dirt surface of Etaa's streets. They kept close to the walls, checking the open doorways before passing each one.

It began to rain, a soft drizzle. The ground beneath their feet turned into a thin mud. Both glanced back to see what happened to the rain on the ruined surface; it hissed and spat pink gas.

"Don't get that stuff wet," O'Neill advised.

"Right," Carter said patiently.

The city was arranged on what Jackson told them was a "kraal" plan, with the city wall defining the perimeter, two or three concentric circles of round mud-thatch houses inside that, and a wide open area in the middle. Each house had its own satellites, for grain storage, cooking, and extended family. The middle, open area was the place that originally held the flocks of the cattle-herding Masai; for the Etaa, it was a marketplace, an occasional corral for the town's more valuable jointly owned livestock, and a dance floor for the frequent celebrations. There had been a jump dance to welcome SG-1 to this world, and a big bonfire with lots of food and music.

Now the central clearing was completely empty, the surrounding houses with their own individual compounds eerily silent.

"You've noticed what I've noticed, I hope?" Carter asked as they checked around a corner.

"Yeah. Where are the bodies?"

"There aren't even any bugs."

There weren't. The last insect they'd seen had dropped from the pink gas outside the town wall.

There weren't any bird-critters, either, or animals, or humans. The place was completely deserted. No chickens or dogs, imported from Earth along with the human population.

"I do not like this," O'Neill asserted with great conviction.

"I do not like this, Sam I am," Carter responded ritually. O'Neill sighed. "Sorry, sir."

"I'm supposed to have the patent on the wiseass remarks, Major," O'Neill snapped. The two of them hadn't even looked at each other during this exchange. "Okay, let's head for the tower and see if there's anything up there. That's where they were supposed to be holding the prisoners."

The path to the tower, unlike the rest of the streets of Etaa, seemed to be newly paved with a shiny asphalt surface. It didn't hiss, not even when O'Neill spat on it, and it failed to dissolve several of the test substances—dirt clod, candy wrapper, MRE—they tossed at it. It had no particular smell. So they proceeded very gingerly down the path, until they arrived at the northernmost of the once-twin towers at the main gate of Etaa. The footing was powdery, slippery underfoot, as if it would be greasy when wet.

The black surface seemed thicker just inside the main gate, and not as shiny; it covered most of the floor and halfway up the walls, in an irregular pattern as if someone had used a paint sprayer. It flaked away from the floor as they walked across it, its consistency somewhere between powder and goo. O'Neill risked touching one of the walls covered with the stuff, and it left a dark smudge across his fingertips and nothing more. It had stopped abruptly just short of the gate itself, and had been invisible from their vantage point outside the town.

"You're *not* going to taste that, sir," Carter informed him even as the thought crossed his mind. She took another vial from her pack—the one containing the melted mud was still intact—and scraped a little of the black stuff into it. O'Neill shrugged and turned away, wiping his fingertips across his fatigue pants and leaving a long black smear in the process.

They made their way up the circular stairs that curved around the inside of the tower walls, stopping an listening at every step. As they proceeded, the black stuff became more patchy. Some of the original stone of the tower—one of the few buildings in the town actually constructed of something other than mud brick, woven vines, and thatch—was still exposed, and the black stood out sharply against the soft pale yellow.

The observation room of the tower, where Morley reported that the SG-4 prisoners had been held, was coated at one end with the black stuff. On the other side of the room, near the window that overlooked the interior of Etaa, the place looked as if a fight had taken place, with low stools overturned, drapes ripped down, rushes on the floor scuffed to reveal bare floor. But there was no sign of life.

O'Neill went to the inner-side window while Carter searched the room. His vantage point overlooked the main street of the town, and he could see most of the main square. There was nothing, not even on the farthest periphery from the melted area. Nothing moved in Etaa. No impossibly tall humans, no animals, no bird-critters. Nothing at all.

He shifted over to the exterior window, searching for and finding the other members of the team moving down the line of the wall, just inside the shelter of the trees. Satisfied that they were all right, he continued to scan the horizon, looking for signs of the tubenecks or their opponents.

"Uh, sir?" Carter said. Her voice sounded odd. "There's something here I think you should look at."

He glanced over to see her squatting beside a ripped length of curtain, balancing against the butt end of her rifle. Taking one last look around, he came over and went down on one knee beside her.

"What is it?"

Carter pointed to the curtain, following its folds until it intersected a particularly thick layer of black stuff. The line where curtain met goo could have been drawn with a straightedge.

O'Neill unlimbered a pocketknife and poked at the black stuff. It didn't cover the curtain—it *was* the curtain. Or it had been, at least.

"Yikes," he muttered. "Where did all this come from?"

"Sir." The blond captain's voice was strangled. "Look."

She was pointing with one unsteady hand at a bit of bright metal similarly cut across by the goo. O'Neill worked his knife blade under the scrap and tenderly worked it free from the fold of cloth that had snagged it. It was machined metal, not something manufactured on Etaa, a smooth, slightly curved plain rectangle about an inch long, with one flange sticking out, trimmed by the goo.

"What—" he began.

"They're captain's bars, sir," Carter said, her tone tight with unshed tears. "Look." She picked up the bit of metal and held it next to the gold leaves on her own shoulder. "This belonged to—" she looked down at the goo—"this *was* Captain Dwyer of SG-4. And look there—"

His gaze followed her pointing finger to a place well above his eye level, where the black stuff had disfigured the cool yellow wall. At the very top of the black mark, as if held in place by it, was a small tuft of white feathers, as if from the very edge of an edge of an elaborate headdress. "All this black stuff, sir—I'm betting it's all carbon. Everything living here is dead. They've all been—" She gestured helplessly at the black layer. "They must have herded everyone onto that street we came down, where it was so thick, and—"

"Which 'they,' Captain? The Jaffa? The tubenecks? The moths?" O'Neill was just as shaken as Carter, and normally he wouldn't have minded if she knew it. But this wasn't the time or place to allow emotion to control their action. They had a military problem with immediate consequences not only to his own team but, very possibly, to Earth itself.

Carter took a very deep breath and let it out slowly. "Unknown, sir. Teal'C may be able to tell us if this was a weapon the Jaffa had under development, but it doesn't match anything I've seen or heard him talk about. There are some similarities between this and the stuff we saw on the battlefield, but as for which side used it—assuming it wasn't something available to both sides—I can't tell.

"It obviously acted quickly and completely. The remnants show that much. Maybe further analysis back home will tell us more."

O'Neill nodded, chewing his lip thoughtfully. "All right, Major. Collect your sample. Until further notice we're going to assume everything left on this planet is an enemy."

Teal'C, Jackson, and Kinsey watched the other two go, and then Teal'C moved farther back into cover. Daniel watched as Kinsey kept his mouth shut and followed, his eyes busy over every detail of the place. Daniel could remember a time, only a few years ago, when he could publish his research findings in peer-reviewed journals and engage in endless academic debate over the interpretation of a variation in heiratic script, with one side holding that the symbol meant something entirely new and subtle and the other that the hapless scribe, three thousand years dead, had been caught at last in a spelling error. That sort of thing happened when one's words literally were written in stone.

Newspapers, though—his professors used to sniff with disdain. Newspapers were created to wrap fish in. Weekly or monthly newsmagazines weren't much different, in their opinion. That sort of thing had no scientific value whatsoever. It added exactly zero to the sum of human knowledge.

Daniel Jackson, Ph.D., wasn't so sure. Opinions mattered much more in the day-to-day world than all the reviewed journals in all the university libraries everywhere. And there were more things in heaven than were dreamt of by all the Doctors of Philosophy in all the universities in the earth.

He shook his head to clear it of such meanderings, and then shook it again to get the lank blond hair out of hie eyes. He needed a haircut again. He would have gotten one if it hadn't been for Carter's racquetball challenge.

He hoped the tapes came out. He wanted to take a good long look at the manipulators on those moth creatures, and he wanted a lot more information about the details of manufacture of the weapons those long-necked beings carried. He could tell quite a lot about a species based on one or two stray items, and could speculate happily about the rest for years. Two new intelligent species on one world!

Or not. One might be from this world—he knew the human community hadn't done much exploration here—and the other from another world. Or they might both be from other worlds. They might use ships, or—no, at least the tubenecks had seemed puzzled by the Gate.

How had they managed to miss the aliens the first time? Didn't the Etaans have any warning at all?

Shostoka'an smiled maternally down at Jack O'Neill. "We are very few," she admitted cheerfully. "We are those of this city, and the outlying places where we find the yellow metal and farm, and that is all. This is a good place, but there does not need to be many of our kind here."

She's passed over a gorgeous cup, roughly inlaid with gems, some of which had no counterpart he knew of on Earth. O'Neill had taken a cautious sniff—he'd learned not to accept proffered food and drink automatically—and made a face.

Daniel had taken it from him, raised it in salute to the tall, elegant woman, and sneaked one preliminary sniff himself before downing the concoction. As he suspected, it was cow's milk, rich and creamy, straight from the udder, mixed with blood, probably from the same cow. It made sense as a ceremonial drink for the Masai. "Thank you," he said, wiping his mouth. "It is good. You have healthy herds."

Shostoka'an nodded in appreciation. "What of your herds on your world? Do they increase?"

"They do. We are fortunate. There are no"—oh, dear, what would the local equivalent of lions be?—"no predators where we come from." He sent a mental apology to the summarily dismissed fanged half of Earth's ecosystem.

"Do you have enemies on this world?" Jack had asked.

Shostoka'an had tilted her head thoughtfully, the ostrichlike plumes waving in the slight breeze. With instinctive courtesy, she hadn't offered Jack a second chance at the blood-and-milk, though Daniel knew Jack would have choked it down somehow if she had. "Enemies? What do you mean?"

"Those that brought you here are your enemies," Teal'C had said.

Shostoka'an had smiled brilliantly, teeth and jewelry gleaming equally in the firelight. "But they have been gone a very, very long time, and never returned. They are all dead now."

And now Shostoka'an and all her people were missing. He wondered if a few remained in the outlying farms and the gold mines, hiding from the disaster that had come to their world.

Teal'C stopped with a wave of the hand. Kinsey moved to the Jaffa's far side, and the three of them looked at more of the ruins of Etaa.

"This is worse than the other side," Kinsey observed.

"No kidding," Daniel agreed, and unlimbered his camcorder to take a quick shot of the vanished sections of city wall and crumbled houses within the inner compounds. He wished he'd brought more tape.

"I do not think there are hostile creatures still in this place," Teal'C said thoughtfully. "But we know they are nearby. We must remain cautious."

"I'll second that," Daniel agreed. "I'd like to get closer, though, and see if I can get better images of some of the damage. The experts back home may be able to tell what kind of weapon did this."

"They have a lot of experience in that sort of thing?" Kinsey inquired.

Jackson shrugged. "Some." Without waiting for Teal'C to comment, he moved forward, out of the shadow of the trees, the camcorder held to his eye as he panned slowly across the shattered stones and wood of the wall and the houses within.

Behind him, he could hear Teal'C's nearly silent grunt of disapproval, and Kinsey's footsteps, following. Teal'C would take up a rearguard position, Jackson knew, keeping an eye out for anything that might menace them.

Out of the corner of his eye he could still see the remaining tower at the main entrance to the town. A flicker of movement jerked his attention toward it, and then he saw Teal'C raise a hand in acknowledgment. O'Neill and Carter, then. Good. He liked knowing where everyone was.

It was odd, he thought, as he approached the breach in the wall; with this much destruction, there ought to be more smell of decay, more bodies—not just that lingering unpleasant scent that was sometimes overwhelmingly there, sometimes not present at all. Maybe the Jaffa had already rounded everyone up before the tubenecks and moths had shown up. He almost hoped so, and then was shocked at himself, at the thought that there might be something even worse than Goa'uld slavery.

He could hear a scrabbling sound coming from behind him and spun around, only to see Kinsey balancing uncertainly on a pile of rubble. Teal'C, behind the journalist, was frowning mightily, probably at the other man's propensity for seeking out the highest point possible. *You'd think a combat reporter would know better*, he thought disgustedly, and then he saw Kinsey's face change and Teal'C bring his energy staff up to firing position. Teal'C was moving very slowly. It wasn't like the Jaffa at all.

He tried to look up, but it was as if he had been caught in molasses. His arms wouldn't lift, and he could barely turn his head from side to side. He was having trouble breathing. He was vaguely aware of a high-pitched whistle.

He could hear loud noises—something beating at the air like giant fans. *Wings*.

A shadow swept over him, and he tried to force his head up to see.

Too late. Long knives stabbed into either side of his body, just under his shoulders, and he was yanked up into the air, his own enhanced weight dragging him against the sharpness that pinned him, as the wings above him snapped downward. The camcorder went spinning down to the ground and bounced. The paralysis, and the whistle, stopped at the same time. He heard the sound of an energy staff being discharged.

He twisted frantically, struggling, and it only drove knives—the talons projecting from the jointed legs of the moth, too similar to that bug that had bitten him earlier to be coincidental—deeper into his flesh. He couldn't lift his arms to strike back, to wield a weapon of his own. As if adding insult to injury, the powder from the moth's wings drifted over him, making him sneeze, and he felt something deep inside his body go *crunch*.

Gusts of wind buffeted him back and forth, but he was past noticing. He had fainted.

CHAPTER SIXTEEN

"Okay, I get the picture," O'Neill said, rising hastily to his feet and giving the captain a hand up. "That's enough. I think it's fair to say that if there are any human survivors on this world, they're going to be hiding too deep for us to find. Let's get the hell out of here, and blow this Gate. I don't know who's fighting who on this world, but we want no part of it. They're not going to follow us home."

Carter swallowed. "Sir, if I may make a suggestion—"

"Make it snappy, Carter."

"I think we ought to show this to Mr. Kinsey. He needs to understand what we're dealing with."

O'Neill glared at her, the kind of glare that indicated that he knew she was right and didn't much like the fact. "All right," he said at last. "But if he doesn't get it, well, too bad. We're not spending one more minute here than we have to. We've got no guarantees those aliens aren't coming back."

"I think they're finished," she said quietly. But O'Neill was already at the observation window.

"Can't see them anymore," he reported. "They've got at least another hour before rendezvous. Let's stay here for another half hour—or until we see more of those things—and then head for the meeting place."

The words were barely out of his mouth before Carter, standing at the cityside window, said sharply,

"Sir. That's Kinsey. And Daniel and Teal'C aren't with him."

Teal'C watched in horror as the bolt of energy from his staff passed harmlessly over the body of the moth. It was flying erratically, weighed down by the body of the archaeologist, its wings straining to lift itself and its prey over the rubble. At unpredictable moments the giant wings would grab more air, causing it to bob up and down, making a second shot extremely risky.

Daniel was impaled on the barbs of a second set of appendages, twisting, writhing. As the moth struggled to lift itself past a roofline, the two watchers saw his body go abruptly limp.

The human journalist was as shocked as he was, Teal'C noted; Kinsey simply showed it more. His face was drained of color, and he was spinning in place, trying to watch all the skies at once for another of the moth creatures.

"Go to the tower and notify O'Neill and Carter," Teal'C said rapidly, already moving at a quick trot toward the house behind which Daniel—and his abductor—had disappeared. "Stay with them. I will recover Daniel Jackson."

Frank Kinsey had absolutely no doubt that the Jaffa meant exactly what he said. He could barely repress the desire to scramble after him, screaming, *"Wait! Stop! Don't leave me here alone with those things!"*

But Teal'C was gone, moving with amazing grace and quickness for such a large man, his energy staff held close to his side.

And Frank Kinsey was all by himself on an alien world where things swooped down from the sky, and he wasn't thinking about headlines anymore.

The tower was to his left, at about ten o'clock. He

began running, stumbling, still twisting his neck to try to watch the skies.

Teal'C pursued the moth creature and its prey with single-minded determination. While it would be good to have Carter and O'Neill to back him up, he felt no particular responsibility to Kinsey. The reporter was expendeable. Daniel Jackson was not.

He lost sight of the winged thing as he entered the streets of Etaa. They weren't streets, really, just wide dirt tracks between the low fences that set off the family compounds from each other. Because the compounds were all roughly circular, the concept of a straight path did not exist in Etaa. Teal'C vaulted some of the fences in his effort to maintain a line on the direction the moth had taken. Such an action should have been greeted with questions, protests— it was very rude not to use the gates. There was nothing, only silence, and an occasional small powdery black splotch against the yellow ground.

Other than that, the place was scrupulously clean. The Etaans did not litter, left no trash to clutter the streets of their home. A large trash pit downwind of the city held the decaying organics that were the refuse of a culture with low technology. The people of this world knew quite a bit about veterinary herbs, a little about smelting, and once they had known nothing at all about Jaffa.

He could hear the sound of his own footsteps on the dry, dusty ground, but nothing else. He stopped to listen.

The window slits in the houses around him were usually covered with thin woven cloth, neatly pinned to the inside wall of the house. Now the coverings were torn loose, flapping out the windows or lying limp on the ground, not even fluttering in the bit of a breeze. The doors, usually open in a sociable society, gaped like dead jaws. Teal'C risked a quick glance inside each large thatched building but didn't bother entering; the moth's wingspan was such that he didn't expect they'd be inclined to take a victim—prisoner? prey?—inside one of the houses.

He was right. He rounded the side of one of the larger family compounds to the central corral and saw the moth—several moths. Several, acting exactly like any army's work detail, were intently tearing apart one of the granary huts; golden and brown grain was already spilling out on the ground at their feet as they fastened their jaws deep into the thatch and pulled. The toughly woven vines gave way as easily as butter.

At one end of the cleared area more moths lay on the ground in a heap. He could detect movement, but had the clear impression they were injured.

At the other end of the clearing was something new, not characteristic of Etaa, a clumsily constructed structure of poles perhaps ten feet high and thirty feet long, holding several large dark cylindrical objects bound in a thick yellow rope

On closer examination he realized that some of the "poles" were actually limbs of—presumably—dead moths. The barbed claws of the legs served to support the construction; the multiple bent joints of the legs contributed to its ramshackle appearance.

That it was a sturdy structure, however, there was no doubt whatsoever. Not only did it support the weight of several other very large objects, but as he watched, the moth used its horizontal jaws to yank its prey off of its own talons. Jackson made no sound and did not resist, flopping limply. The moth heaved his body up, carefully hung Daniel Jackson on one of the projecting hooks, and began wrapping him in ropes of thick yellow silk spun from its own body.

Kinsey couldn't see the tower from the depths of the town, but he had the general direction and considerable motivation. As he ran he kept looking over his shoulder until he tripped yet again, and then he put his head down and started watching where he put his feet.

In a few minutes he found himself slipping on a layer of black that covered much of the street before him. He had almost fallen, and had paused to try to catch his balance, when he looked up to catch a glimpse of patterned brown wings lifting over him. He scrambled into a nearby doorway, out of sight, and leaned against the wall, panting heavily.

He could still hear the ominous flap of wings overhead, and tried to hold his breath. It did no good; he had run too far and too fast not to try to pull air into his lungs. He settled for breathing through his mouth until he could control the frantic gasping. By that time the thump of wings against air had faded away. He spared a glance around the interior of the house: bedding area, firepit, a rack of interlaced rods holding something woven, a child's doll.

He picked it up to look more closely.

It was a simple carved doll, with sticks for arms and legs, two eyes gouged into the soft wood and a wide smile underneath. A scrap of rough red cloth was carefully knotted around its waist for clothing; a short piece of string hung around its neck for a necklace.

It was the first evidence he had seen, other than the houses, that there were actual people, human beings, here; and even that had been difficult to grasp, because the doors were taller than he was used to and the windows set higher in the walls. But the doll looked exactly like dozens he had seen in the poorer areas of the American South and in villages in the Baltic and out in the Australian bush. Strictly home-made and much loved by some child who was no longer around anywhere.

Humans on other worlds are much the same as they are here on Earth. Children play with dolls—

There was no time to search the place. Listening, he couldn't hear the telltale sound of tripartite wings any longer, and so he peeked out the door. Nothing, no one was around. Not even the moths.

He was more cautious then about moving from place to place, looking for signs of the other aliens as well, expecting at any moment to see triangular mantis heads at the end of long, flexible necks peering over a thatched roof at him. The tubenecks, after all, had some kind of flame-throwing, projectile weaponry, while he wasn't sure *what* kind of weapons the moths wielded. He'd seen both Jackson and Teal'C held in some kind of paralysis while the moth had descended to take its prey, so they had to have something.

But as far as he could see, the tubenecks were all outside the city, while the moths held the inside; perhaps that was why the tubenecks had responded first to the sound of the Gate being activated.

That didn't mean they couldn't attack without warning. He decided to keep an eye out for them as well, just in case. At least the damn things couldn't fly. He hoped.

He ducked from circular building to circular building, moving toward the city wall until he could see the single remaining intact guard tower, perhaps two and a half "normal" stories tall. O'Neill had mentioned something about tall people on this world, and their homes were proportional.

He debated about whether to call out to attract the attention of the other members of the team. He had no way of knowing what the moths could hear, and he didn't want to attract their attention and end up impaled like Jackson. He didn't think he'd ever forget the sagging body swinging from the curved, eight-inch barbs, or the slowly blossoming dark stains that spread from the top of the man's fatigues where the hooks held him in place beneath his captor's abdomen. The memory made him abandon strict caution.

"O'Neill!" Kinsey called hoarsely as he arrived at the bottom of the tower, trying simultaneously to keep his voice down and project it.

He ran for the steps and nearly tumbled in his haste to get through the door. He had barely managed to pick himself up, wiping the ubiquitous greasy black powder off his hands, when O'Neill appeared in the doorway from the floor above.

"Don't shoot!"

O'Neill was already raising his weapon to point at the roof.

"It's Jackson. The moths got him, picked him up and carried him off, your buddy went after him, sent me—"

For a moment shock held O'Neill still, as if he were torn between two decisions.

"Get up here," O'Neill said at last, his face pale. "I want you to see something, and then we're outta here. Save your questions until later."

Kinsey looked around, confused, scraping black powder off the soles of his shoes. "What is it?" he demanded. "What are you going to show me? What's more important than—"

"Carter, brief him. And *make* it brief."

Carter stepped forward and led the journalist over to the inner-side window, pointing out the broad black path that cut the town in half. Meanwhile, O'Neill assembled her gear and his own and did a careful check from both windows.

"Yeah, I saw that stuff. What is it? It's all over everything."

"We believe it's all that remains of everything that lived here," she said. "Look at this curtain."

Then she showed him the bit of metal. "The Etaans didn't have the capability to process metal to this extent," Carter informed him. "This had to be from one of our people." She held the scrap to her shoulder, showing him the damaged insignia next to the complete one representing one rank higher.

To his credit, Kinsey grasped the implications only a second later. "What kind of weapon could—could *carbonize* people so completely? There aren't even any bone fragments," he asked. "And the stuff it didn't touch, like that curtain—it looks completely undamaged, but a centimeter away it's just not there anymore. What did this?"

By that time O'Neill was down the steps and out the door, and Carter made it clear that there was no more time for questions as she followed him. It was irrelevant anyway, at least to the crisis at the moment. They had more important problems to deal with.

"You were working over to the north," O'Neill said. "Which way did it take him from there?"

Kinsey opened his mouth and shut it again, temporarily unable to distinguish compass points. O'Neill was watching, the fire in his eyes beginning to erupt from smolder to flames. Kinsey realized abruptly that he was dealing with a very dangerous, and very, very angry man. The graying colonel was not about to surrender one of his own without a fight.

"It went into the town," he said at last. "It carried him in. Your guy, the, uh, alien—"

"His name is *Teal'C*," Carter snapped.

Kinsey swallowed. "Teal'C. He followed it, him. Jackson was hurt."

"Bad?" Both team members were completely focused on him.

Kinsey nodded. "Real bad."

"Keep up and keep quiet."

And keep out of my way, Kinsey silently finished the instructions. He couldn't think of anything he wanted more.

CHAPTER SEVENTEEN

They spread out, circling separate family compounds rather than keeping together and narrowing the scope of their search. It meant that the three of them were out of each other's sight for a considerable interval, but they covered much more ground that way, and at the moment O'Neill was more interested in covering ground than imperfect safety. He remembered all too well what those claws on the moth's legs had looked like. And wasn't it just like Daniel to take point and then get distracted by some bit of unusual cultural artifact, forgetting everything he knew about staying alert? The scientist was a good fighter when he had to be, but deep down in his soul he'd rather have his nose in a book.

He would not allow himself to think about Daniel as a friend just now. He was an objective, and they would by God achieve that objective and take him home with them. Period.

They met Teal'C on their way to the central market. Carter sighted him first and whistled sharply to attract the attention of the others. The Jaffa jerked his energy staff into the ready position at the sound and then put it up as he recognized the people converging on him. He looked somewhat worried, O'Neill noted, which meant that for Teal'C he was most likely frantic. This was not a good sign.

"There are seven of the flying beings in one of the

secondary kraals," the Jaffa reported. "They have four captives, including one of the other aliens. All but Daniel appear to be dead. The flying creatures do not seem to know what to make of the human victims."

"Lead on."

"We also experienced some kind of effect that could have been the force field Major Morley described," the Jaffa went on as they jogged steadily deeper into the city. Teal'C's sense of direction was unerring as he led them through one family compound after another. O'Neill was beginning to feel like he was running the hurdles, given the number of fences they crashed over. The Jaffa wasn't even out of breath. "It was associated with a high-pitched sound."

"You think it could be mechanical?" Carter asked as they slowed at last. Her voice was very low, could barely be heard at a distance of six feet.

"No. It seemed to be made by the creature itself. I saw no machines."

"Probably evolved as a way to paralyze prey."

It was more evidence that the fliers were on an even lower level technologically than the Etaans, too, O'Neill thought. That argued that they were actually native to this world. That the Etaans had simply never before encountered them in all the hundreds of years they'd occupied the planet was sheer luck. In O'Neill's experience a lot of good luck like that eventually turned bad.

Only a few minutes later, they were gathered at a vantage point that allowed them to see the moth compound.

Teal'C had said the flying creatures didn't know what to make of humans. Watching the activities of the moths around the kraal, O'Neill had to agree. One tubeneck hung on what looked like a drying rack, next to a cow; two Etaans; and Daniel. The others were obviously dead, with gaping holes through which they could see bones, internal organs, fatty tissue. O'Neill chose not to believe that Daniel was too, though there was an awful stillness to the younger man. What O'Neill could see of Jackson's face was white as a sheet. He was trussed awkwardly in gelantinous-looking yellow bonds, hanging like a suit of clothes tossed onto a hook, his jacket soaked with blood that had flowed down almost to his knees. They had to get him out of there fast before he simply bled to death, but at least he hadn't yet been gutted.

Having identified his target, he surveyed the enemy troops.

Two of the moths were obviously injured, dragging ragged wings and broken limbs behind them as they crawled across the open space toward the shelter of one of the huts. Two of the other five appeared to be conferring, standing almost upright with wings spread, heads spinning back and forth as they tapped each other on the thorax area with their first pair of legs. The other three were busy dismantling what had once been a nearly-full granary, packing grain into body pouches.

Carter was running the camcorder again, focusing on each alien in turn. "Do you think this is an indigenous species, sir?" she asked softly, her words obscured by the recorder held to her eye. "I don't see much sophistication in anything here."

"We don't know," O'Neill said harshly. "It may not have to be sophisticated to do the kind of damage we saw. Teal'C, that black stuff we've been seeing is the remains of the Etaans. We're not sure how, but they were reduced to carbon, and from the looks of it, it happened incredibly fast. Tell me the Goa'uld don't have this one."

"They do not," the Jaffa confirmed. "I have not seen this effect before. I think even Apophis would have second thoughts about confronting a race with such power, even if they are otherwise primitive."

"Oh, *peachy*. That's all we need. More incredibly powerful alien races that don't like us."

"Well, we don't *know* that they don't like us," Kinsey said, as if trying desperately to find a reasonable, positive note somewhere. He too was a bit pale, and looking anywhere but at the scene in the kraal in front of them. "I know this is horrible, but—but they don't even know us. It could all be a mistake."

O'Neill gave him an icy look. "You know what? I don't *care*. I don't like *them*. We're not going to wait around to find out whether or not this was just a giant misunderstanding—a few thousand people lived in this town, and so far as I can tell they're *all dead*. And *we* are going to get Daniel out of there and cut and run. Starting immediately."

"How?" Kinsey said, still being reasonable. But O'Neill had turned away, deliberately putting the journalist out of his mind, while he worked on solving that very problem.

Their vantage point was inside the kraal fence, on the other side of one of the secondary houses. Holes had been ripped through the thatch, making it easy to see what was going on. Carter had wormed her way into the house itself and was getting tape as near the aliens as possible.

Suddenly she checked herself in the middle of one of her sweeps of the compound and wriggled back to the rest of them. "Daniel, sir. He's coming to. He's alive."

Jackson was definitely still alive—they could see him moving feebly, hear him groaning as he regained consciousness. An unexpected wave of relief washed over O'Neill. At least Daniel hadn't been injected with something paralyzing and set aside for later dining delectation. Or maybe he had and the stuff just didn't work on humans. Whatever. The other victims were dead. Daniel really was alive, they had proof, and a part of his mind was profoundly grateful, and profoundly determined to keep the young scientist that way.

As Carter returned to her filming, Teal'C moved over to Kinsey and tapped him on the shoulder. The reporter jumped, startled. Teal'C silently indicated the pack on the other man's back and then pointed to the fence behind them. After a moment of cross-purposes, Kinsey helped the Jaffa remove the pack and watched in fascinated amazement as the three-foot-long backpack unfolded and transformed into a seven-foot-long transport sled. Without saying a word, the Jaffa lifted the sled over the low fence and began moving it around the compound, toward the rack upon which Daniel hung, moaning softly now as he twisted helplessly against his bonds.

"I need flamethrowers," O'Neill muttered under his breath, moving up beside Carter. The two moths that had been communicating with each other in the center of the kraal seemed to have finished their discussion and chittered orders of some kind to the three looting the grain bin. The two injured aliens had crawled to the base of one of the living huts, gouging deep scars in the ground as they used their claws to drag themselves along. Their brown-and-black wings blended neatly against the mud and thatch, providing excellent camouflage.

"Deb didn't pack them," Carter informed him, keeping her voice low even though the moths didn't seem to be able to detect the sound of their voices. "They'll be on the next list, though." Evidently satisfied that she had enough data—or having finally exhausted her supply of tape—she put away the camcorder and unslung her rife. "But that's a great idea. For next time."

"It is?" O'Neill asked. Then an unholy gleam came into his eye. "Yes, it is. I like it. Teal'C!" The Jaffa vaulted the kraal fence and joined them. "You've got the sled out—good. You and Kinsey circle around and get into position as close to Daniel as you can. Carter, you go with them and cover their backs. I'm going to create a diversion. Wait for it, then get Daniel down and out and back to the Gate as fast as you can and don't stop for anything. I'll keep them busy and follow as fast as I can."

"What if . . ." Kinsey began.

O'Neill cut him off. "There is no 'try,' grasshopper. Do it."

"He really mixes his pop references when he's under stress," Carter murmured.

"Smart-ass." But they were already moving, fading out the back of the ruined hut and over the fence, working their way around the compound in opposite directions.

So this is what the Lakota Sun Dance actually feels like, Daniel thought through a haze of shock. The catching-barbs on the moth's legs had pierced just under the clavicles in front and through the broad muscles of the shoulder in back; in fact he was fairly sure one barb had punched a hole through the infra-spinous fossa of his left scapula. Fortunately or otherwise, when they'd hung him up to dry, they'd mistaken his fatigues for skin. He could feel the smooth surface of the hook against his back, and the weight of his own body—plus the extra gravity of this world— dragging against the armholes of his jacket.

But there was no pain. Or at least, no immediate pain. Pain was out there somewhere on the horizon but hadn't settled in for a visit just yet.

Somehow he had managed to hang on to his glasses. They didn't seem to be doing him much good, with half his vision obscured by a mist of condensation and an uncharacteristic inability to focus. He could see large things moving around, more or less at eye level. If he looked down at himself, he could see sticky yellowish ropes holding his arms to his sides. He could also see the dark, soaked surface of his heavy jacket, sodden clear to the waist and below with blood, smell it all over.

Uh-oh, he thought muzzily. *That's not good.*

A wave of dizziness washed over him, and his head rolled. One of the moth creatures dragged itself over to him. He tried to concentrate on it, make mental notes about how it moved, how many limbs it had, the facets of its eyes, the odd smell of it. Useless. He peered at it and it blurred. The only thing he could see at all clearly was the curved spike on one leg, which it was holding up to him as if to show him his own blood, or perhaps the crack along the tip of the shaft. Look what you did, it seemed to say. What do you think you are, anyway?

More than you bargained for, you bastard, he thought.

The moth turned away to one of the other victims and began slapping the side of one clawed limb against it, rocking the entire structure. It wasn't clear what, if anything, the alien thought it was accomplishing, but the movement hurt. Daniel gasped in agony and sank into the comforting darkness once again.

"How can I help?" Kinsey asked as they moved around the perimeter of the family compound. "What do you want me to do?"

"We're going to get him down and put him on the sled," Carter said. She didn't bother to look at him as she talked; she and Teal'C were busy keeping an eye out for moths, tubenecks, and anything else that might sight them and sound an alarm. "You get to pull."

"I can do that." It was the best use of his abilities they could have come up with, he realized. A neat and cleanly distinguished division of duties.

Carter glanced over to him then and smiled briefly

at him, an uncanny flash of sunlight in a dire situation. "Teal'C will help."

They had maneuvered to the back of the rack on which the moths' victims hung. The three scavengers were crouching in the middle of the cleared area, their bodies distended with the grain that crammed every available crevice and cavity.

"It looks like they're getting ready to take off," Carter murmured. "Damn, I wish I could record this."

"Give me the camera," Kinsey suggested. "I'd kind of rather you concentrated on firepower."

"Just don't lose the tapes." The three of them pressed against the back of the rack, trying to keep out of sight as the scavengers rose in the air.

Kinsey managed to load the last new tape and have the recorder up and running in time to catch the second moth launching itself, heaving its burden of stolen grain awkwardly against gravity. For a few long moments he wondered whether the alien would actually be able to take to the air, but then the wings lifted and curled, cupping the wind, and it staggered into the sky.

Across the cleared area, he could see something moving behind the hut where the injured moths lay atop each other.

The third scavenger moth forced its awkward way into the sky, leaving the two casualties and the two able-bodied ones he couldn't help but think of as leaders.

Teal'C and Carter had moved the sled into position behind the structure of poles that held the victims. Kinsey shut down the camera, securing the last tape in one of the pockets low on the legs of his fatigues, and watched as Carter, the lightest of them, climbed up the back of the pole structure, combat knife in hand. The rack swayed back and forth, and for one heart-stopping moment he was afraid the whole thing was going to come crashing down. Apparently Carter thought so too; she froze halfway up, waiting until the structure regained its stability. Kinsey could see the side of Daniel Jackson's face through the latticework. Miraculously, through everything, he had managed to retain his glasses.

Carter was probing carefully through the lattice of wood, vines, and dismembered insect limbs at the yellow ropes that bound Jackson. The blade stuck against the yellow ligament, and she cursed softly as she tried to twist it free.

Jackson came to abruptly and flung his head back, his teeth bared with a rush of agony.

"Daniel, it's okay. We're here, we're going to get you out of here." Carter's words were soft and hurried. She had one arm hooked around a strut, her toes stuck into crevices of the framework, and the whole thing swayed as she tugged the knife free and tried again.

"Sam?" He could feel the barb digging between his shoulders. It was a welcome distraction from the fire that devoured them.

"Yeah, Danny." She paused to look across the compound. If O'Neill was going to do something spectacular, this would be a really good time for it. The yellow stuff wasn't going to give way; it stretched under the blade of her knife, stuck to the metal. "It's me, Daniel. It's going to be okay."

He was held to the rack by one of the insect hooks. She could see where the fabric of his jacket strained upward against the barb, but she couldn't tell if it was dragging his skin as well. She slipped the knife back into her boot and tried to pull the shirt free from his belt without moving him. Daniel sucked in his breath.

"Sorry, sorry," she whispered. Glancing down, she could see Teal'C maintaining a steady scan of the area around and above them, staff at the ready, and

Kinsey alternating between staring anxiously up at her and looking around frantically. Returning her attention to the problem of getting Daniel loose, she looked down the rack below him. There were a number of wicked-looking hooks set and ready to snag any body sliding downward. "Oh, shit."

"Unnerstatemt," Daniel muttered. Despite herself, Carter chuckled, and for the first time began to think that this situation might come out all right after all.

Across the compound, Jack O'Neill had pulled most of the wall away from the back end of the hut and piled it loosely against the front side next to the door. Through the opening of the door he could see the expanse of one of the moths' wings, a smooth surface that looked almost like velvet, the pattern of colors softer and more subtle than was apparent from a distance. This particular wing was torn across, and through it he could see a segmented leg with a series of ivory-white hooks in successively smaller sizes extending down its length. The leg shifted, and he held his breath, but the moths seemed oblivious to the sound and movement only inches away from them.

Across the compound he could see Daniel flinging his head back. Behind him he caught a glimpse of blonde hair—Carter.

He pulled out a lighter from his pocket and snapped the striker. It had been a long time since he'd smoked, but it held memories he wasn't willing to surrender just yet. Besides, it was too useful a tool to discard entirely. A tongue of flame flared into life.

As Carter watched, a wisp of smoke rose from the round building against which the crippled aliens lay. By the time the two leaders had noticed it, clear yellow tongues of flame were licking at the thatch of the roof and the walls.

The fire spread with amazing rapidity, and Carter

muttered unladylike comments under her breath as she tried again to cut the yellow ropes. When her efforts failed again, she cursed and slid one hand through the shirt where the hook had penetrated. "Sorry, Danny," she whispered, feeling her way along the barb to Daniel's back. He cried out as she touched the sodden, cold T-shirt and then his mangled muscles. The smell of blood nearly choked her. "Sorry, sorry," she repeated in an endless soothing murmur, and continued grimly maneuvering the knife to cut him free.

Across the compound, a bundle of smoldering thatch slid off the roof and directly onto the wings of one of the injured moths, and it rose up and screamed thinly as it caught fire and stumbled into its companion.

The two leaders launched themselves, hovering over the flames, diving through the spiraling gray smoke, the beating of their frantic wings only feeding the fire. Kinsey looked up to see Carter using a lighter to burn away the last of the yellow strands, and then Jackson's body collapsed, sliding unevenly down the rack, and hit the ground, boneless as a bag of winter wheat.

Carter leaped down beside Teal'C, who was already lifting the once-again-unconscious body as if it weighed nothing, as if it were a sleeping child's, and laying it in the light metal shed. The burning moths were screaming at an almost ultrasonic pitch. Teal'C and Kinsey threw themselves against the tow ropes, and the sled began to move as Carter backed behind them, Teal'C's energy staff at the ready.

One of the moths caught sight of them and shrieked.

SG-1 and their guest ran for their lives. Twenty yards to the rear, and gaining rapidly, O'Neill crossed the open compound, ignoring the writhing, burning moths, and followed them.

They paused for just a moment in the giant arch that was the gate of the city, and in that moment the alien was abruptly closer, a shower of dust flaking from dull gray double wings whose span covered at least twenty feet. It braked in midair at the sight of them, rising and falling rather than hovering in one place, its wings making a muted thunder. They could clearly see the dark-red sphincter in its underside opening and closing.

"Good grief, it really *is* Mothra," O'Neill muttered, raising his rifle. Carter tossed the energy staff back to Teal'C and unlimbered her own rifle.

The alien pulled up then, made a staticky noise, and dived on them, the sphincter spraying as it came. The liquid was thick, viscous, and black, and where it touched, what it touched, turned dark and melted, bubbling. A glob hit O'Neill's rifle, and he watched in amazement as the barrel melted off cleanly and dripped onto the ground. Casting the useless weapon aside, he pulled his sidearm and kept on fighting.

Teal'C, O'Neill, and Carter were all firing, even as they pulled back behind the shelter of the gate. Carter was the only one using a standard military-issue automatic rifle, Kinsey noted, but Teal'C fired his staff at the thing, and unlike the bullets, the bolt of energy released by the Jaffa weapon seemed to have an effect. Half of the creature's upper right wing disintegrated, and it spiraled downward to the earth, shrieking thinly. "That's the paralysis sound!" Kinsey yelled, as O'Neill began moving in slow motion.

"I think it's trying to communicate with its friends," Carter said grimly as she too began to slow.

"I agree," Teal'C responded from farther away, and fired again at the alien, blowing the rest of its head off. The sound stopped. So did the paralysis.

"Then I think we'd better haul out of here, don't you?" O'Neill asked, and suited his actions to his words. Rather than heading straight across the battle plain to the Stargate, however, he followed the original path, heading to the outcrop of rock, the sled with the unconscious Jackson bouncing behind them.

"What the hell?" Kinsey panted. "Why are we taking a detour?"

"The F.R.E.D. is there," Carter said. "There's some stuff we need in it."

"What—what kind of stuff? Why can't we just jump through the hoop and g-get h-home?"

"Because we can't be sure these aliens, or the other ones, aren't able to determine the last code entered on the Dial-Home Device. If they can, they'll have the coordinates for Earth."

Kinsey had to envy the captain, who managed to talk without panting while moving at a very brisk, businesslike trot. "But they'll catch us!"

"Well, yeah, if you keep talking!" O'Neill snapped from behind them. "Save your breath and *move!*"

Around him, the members of SG-1 lowered their heads and ran, making no attempt to keep to the cover of the vine-trees now. It took something less than half the time to return to the rock outcrop as it had to make the journey from it to Etaa, and Kinsey was shuddering for breath as the team threw itself on the peacefully parked mechanical puppy.

Trying to make himself useful, Kinsey climbed up on a handy rock and looked around, only to find himself nose to something with a tubeneck, its horizontal jaws working. With a startled cry he fell backward, neatly clearing a line of fire for Teal'C, who blew the triangular head off.

"Okay, got it," Carter said rapidly. Teal'C started down the slope with the sled, Kinsey scrambling to catch up and take the second tow rope. Seconds later the packs were loaded onto the F.R.E.D. and O'Neill was making a last-minute adjustment to the machine.

"Okay, *run!*" he yelled and leaped off the rock outcrop.

They were already running. The sled, made of some light metal, slid easily across the ground, somehow managing not to catch on the vines and the bodies. The weight of the injured man was barely noticeable once they got it moving. It was certainly easier to travel without being weighed down by sixty pounds of pack, adjusted for local gravity. Kinsey felt he was flying along the edge of the bubbled-over battleground, actually leaping alien corpses at full stride.

Then the percussion of the exploding F.R.E.D. hit, and he really was flying for several feet. It was something of a relief to realize he wasn't the only one who had been picked up and tossed through the air; the rest of the team were spitting dirt too. He looked back over his shoulder to see four or five tubenecks not far from the former rock outcrop also picking themselves up, and two moth aliens still pinwheeling through the sky.

By the time they reached the last line of trees before the Gate, both sets of aliens were in pursuit, apparently having set aside their differences in order to deal with the humans. The moths weren't yet close enough to spray, but the tubenecks had some short-range weapons that spat sharply and turned the near ground into an unpleasantly familiar bubbling mass.

O'Neill reached the DHD first and began slapping coordinates on the domed surface. Teal'C and Carter took up positions on either side of him, guarding the route to the Gate. Kinsey shouldered the tow rope and dragged the sled as close to the Gate as he dared, then looked around again to find, first, a tubeneck rapidly gaining on him and second, O'Neill right beside him. The colonel was deliberately slowing his pace to that of the sled.

The wormhole roared open.

It was still fifty feet away, and the tubeneck was only thirty.

O'Neill grabbed one of the ropes, helping to pull Daniel along, while Teal'C and Carter fired steadily at the tubeneck, which was weaving back and forth and returning fire. Then Carter stopped and knelt by the Gate. Three heartbeats later she rose and waved her arms in an all-clear gesture.

"Go!" O'Neill roared, rolling away from Kinsey and then standing, yelling, to draw fire. Carter backed through the Gate. The sled caught, and Jackson moaned as it wobbled, nearly toppling over. Teal'C ran up to Kinsey and took the rope, hauling the sled up and over the rim of the wormhole. Kinsey tried to get up and untangle himself, but his foot slipped on the gravel on the base of the Gate and he fell to one knee.

They were close now, within touching distance of the steps to the Gate, when a shadow crossed above them. Without thinking, Kinsey threw himself to one side, into O'Neill, knocking both of them sprawling across the steps, and at the same time something very, very cold touched Frank Kinsey's left foot, barely missing the sled. He found himself staring at the base of the Stargate, at what looked very much like an impressive mass of C-4 with a very short delay.

O'Neill scrambled to his feet, and Kinsey tried to follow as the colonel stood by, providing covering fire. His foot wouldn't give him any purchase. Bewildered, he glanced down.

It wasn't there.

The next thing he knew, he was thrown bodily into the silver shimmer of the Stargate and falling through a cold that wasn't quite enough to mask that other cold that still possessed him.

CHAPTER EIGHTEEN

"So," O'Neill said, two days later when Frank Kinsey had been released from Medical long enough to visit Hammond's office. The reporter was on crutches. Eventually he would graduate to a cane—he still had half a foot left. He looked wryly at O'Neill, who was spotless and superb in dress blues, seated to one side of the general's desk. Hammond himself was sitting back watchfully, letting O'Neill do the talking for the time being. Kinsey lowered himself carefully into a chair and set his crutches to one side.

"Tell me again about the people's right to know— and tell me what happens when they find out," O'Neill continued. "Tell me what all the conspiracy theorists are going to do, what your dear old dad will do, when they hear you tell them that Earth is only one very small spot in a very big universe. What will all the decent, rational, fair-minded citizens of the world do when you try to give them a whole new perspective on their daily lives?"

Kinsey pulled another chair over and propped what was left of his heavily bandaged foot upon it. He shook his head, ignoring the question for the time being. "Is Dr. Jackson going to be all right?"

"He's going to be in physical therapy for a while." Janet Frasier, sitting at the other end of the desk, was smiling as she closed her clipboard. "Apparently he *was* injected with some kind of venom, but it's a compound native to Etaa and the effect was negligible—anesthetic, if anything. His injuries are pretty serious, but he should eventually regain full range of motion in his shoulders."

"Thanks. I'm glad to hear it." He closed his eyes, still remembering for some reason the contrast of a smear of blood against the utter paleness of Jackson's face. It was an easier image to hold than some of the others. "What about the paralysis field? Is that going to have any effect?"

"None that we can determine. There are no residual aftereffects. So far as I can tell from what you've all told me, it had something to do with the effect of the sound the moths made upon the human brain. Unfortunately the recording quality of the camcorders wasn't quite up to reproducing the effect."

They had tumbled back to Earth only to be pounced upon by a well-trained horde of medical personnel. He'd found himself on a table next to Jackson, had an opportunity to see for himself the shredded gore of Jackson's torso. He'd been grateful to whatever powers there were that the man was unconscious, and wondered how he had managed to keep his lungs intact to breathe. Then the doctors had closed in around him and he hadn't seen Jackson anymore.

"Well, Mr. Kinsey, do you see why we insist that the Stargate project remains secret?" Hammond inquired gently.

"Fire in the crowded theater," Kinsey said softly. "Panic. Distrust. All those things humanity does best."

Hammond smiled thinly. "That matches our own assessment."

O'Neill took up the thread. "Give us time to allow the teams to carry out our missions of threat assessment and discovering ways to protect Earth. Give us a chance to prepare a defense. In a war, you don't take a vote on how to proceed. War isn't a democratic process, not if you want to survive. You limit your complications, and you follow orders."

"Speaking of following orders," Hammond said grimly, addressing O'Neill, "I do recall ordering you to make sure our guest didn't get hurt. You were supposed to show him consequences, not let him suffer them."

O'Neill sat up straighter in his chair, ready to protest.

"Wait a minute," Kinsey interrupted, looking around at the three officers and wondering how his father had managed to survive a full-court press. "I'm not sure I completely agree yet that the public doesn't have a right to know the details, but I know where you're coming from. And anyway, I'm not sure anyone would believe me. Even with this"—he pointed to his injury—"it's just not believable. Praying mantises and giant moths that turn people instantly into greasy black powder? If you think I'm going to put my name on that kind of article, you have another think coming. They'd cart me off to the funny farm. No, General.

"Going through the Gate like that—I don't know. I could have written about all this, maybe, if I hadn't done that. It's almost credible up until you really do it—then it's just, I don't know, science fiction." He paused and smiled wryly at O'Neill. "But now I've got some idea of what you're up against, and what you're willing to do to fight it. So you don't have to worry about me. I'm not going to say anything to anybody, at least for the time being. Not even to dear old Dad."

"That'll drive him nuts," O'Neill remarked.

"Yeah, won't it?" Kinsey grinned.

"Good," Hammond said, slapping his hand on the desk as if finalizing a deal. "And you'll let me know if you change your mind."

"Oh, definitely," Kinsey replied, with a small smile.

"I think I'd like to go lie down again," he went on, and Harriman stepped forward to escort him back to Medical. Frasier followed them out the door.

O'Neill and Hammond were left alone in the general's office. O'Neill got up and opened a cabinet, revealing a decanter of whiskey and a set of cut crystal glasses. Cassidy and Pace were not the only ones who had emergency reserves.

Hammond shared a wry glance with O'Neill as the colonel handed him a half-full glass. "It worked this time," Hammond said. "But I don't think we'll ever pull a stunt like that again."

O'Neill heaved a sigh of relief and the two of them clinked glasses. "You're a good judge of character," he remarked. "I wasn't sure it would work. Especially when we almost lost Daniel." He took a healthy slug of liquor. "But he pitched in. I'm not sure we would have made it back without his help."

"That *wasn't* in the plan."

"Er, no sir. Especially the part about Daniel." O'Neill started to take another drink, looked at the glass thoughtfully, and set it aside. "And what about our friend Samuels?"

"I have plans for Bert Samuels," Hammond growled. "He's going to find himself on TDY. Very long term TDY. In a very, very cold place."

Jack O'Neill smiled.

Late that afternoon, Hammond's driver was standing by to open the door of the sedan and take him away from Cheyenne Mountain. As he settled in on the backseat with his briefcase full of reports, he wondered once again whether he should go ahead and take retirement. He could throw a steak on the grill and plant irises, sit back and have a drink, improve his golf game. Command, after all, wasn't what it was cracked up to be.

But within a few minutes, as the blue sedan wound its way down Cheyenne Mountain, he was deep in studying the preliminary reports on possible new destinations for Stargate missions. O'Neill was right. It *was* a war, for Earth's very survival, and like O'Neill and the rest he was signed up for the duration, even if—if they were lucky—the world never knew.

Don't Miss the Next Explosive Stargate SG-1!
The Morpheus Mandate

Coming Soon

"If it's Tuesday, it must be P4V-837," Jack O'Neill announced as SG-1 stepped through the gate. "Temperature balmy, skies blue, gravity norm—*Hey!*"

Across a lovely meadow, a massive cottonwood tree heaved its roots free of the earth and shook the dirt loose.

"What the—" The four members of SG-1 stood at the foot of the little hill that marked the Stargate on this world and stared as the tree's branches rattled against each other.

A shadow passed between the team and the sun, chilling them to the bone, and Daniel Jackson looked up.

"Uh, Jack. That's a roc, Jack. That's a really, really, *really* big roc."

"That's a bird." Samantha Carter gripped her automatic rifle tensely, watching as the shadow flapped its wings with the sound of thunder. It wheeled above them and swooped down to snatch up the cottonwood in one impossibly huge claw. The sixty-foot tree was the size of a twig in the creature's foot.

"No, it's definitely a roc," Daniel assured her.

"I thought that was something out of mythology," O'Neill said nervously, looking around for the DHD while at the same time keeping an eye on the tree thrashing frantically in the clutches of a bird the size of a small mountain. The bird had a large, curved beak and brilliantly green feathers that could be used to roof houses. It also had very impressive claws.

"It is," Daniel agreed.

"Then what is it doing here?" Teal'C asked as the bird launched itself back into the sky. "And how can it fly?"

"Ask a bumblebee," Jack said. The DHD was perhaps sixty feet away. Behind them, the Gate closed.

The next tree over began to shrug back and forth, tugging its roots free from the bank of earth by the stream.

"Was there *anything* in the M.A.L.P. data that mentioned this?" Carter asked plaintively.

"Uh, not that I saw."

"Me either."

"It was not in my copy of the briefing report."

"Is it just me, or is that tree trying to chase us?"

"I don't know about the tree, Colonel, but those spiders are definitely heading our way."

"I don't think those are technically spiders—"

"I don't care! Get them *off* me!"

"Normally," O'Neill said, batting frantically at the waves of multilegged organisms tickling their way up his pants legs, "I'd say we have a duty to explore this planet, fulfill our mission, and report back. Under the circumstances—" he ducked away from an aggressive swipe by a branch six inches in diameter—"I suggest we let the machines gather more data. . . ."

"Oh, *please* make that an order, sir—"

"Signal to open the iris already sent," Jackson reported, kicking at a tree trunk trying to get between him and the DHD. "Entering—"

And it was gone.

The tree he'd just bruised his foot on vanished. He wiggled his toes—yes, they still hurt like hell.

The bugs were gone too.

The circling rocs overhead, the thrashing trees, the waves of almost-spiders were all gone.

The four of them stood alone in a lovely meadow beside the DHD, not far from the Stargate, and spun in place, trying to see all around themselves and up in the sky at the same time.

Meadow. Tall cottonwoods, waving gently in the breeze. Soft spongy grayish-green grass underfoot, looking remarkably like Bermuda, dotted with little starlike purple and yellow flowers. Puffy white clouds high in the sky. The brooding stone circle of the Stargate, and the dome of the DHD.

Waves splashing on a beach that hadn't been there moments before.

The four of them. And that was all.

"Uh. Did anyone else see—could we have all hallu-cinated—"

"I do not believe it was a hallucination, Daniel Jackson." Teal'C was frowning at a welt on the back of one hand.

"Well, my toes don't think so either, but I could have kicked the Dial-Home Device."

O'Neill shook his head, as if to get the remaining spiders out of his military-trimmed hair. "I don't re-member seeing a large body of water reported," he stated, glaring ominously at a tangle of black-and-yellow kelp washing ashore. He sniffed deeply. "It didn't smell like this a little while ago, either." A gull swooped by. It was a distinctly ordinary-sized bird. O'Neill strode over to the kelp, splashing the shallow shifting water hard with his combat boots. It was real, as real as soaked socks could get.

"I didn't think cottonwoods would grow around saltwater," Carter said doubtfully, eyeing the now-benign trees.

"Perhaps these persons can explain," Teal'C suggested.

The other three members of SG-1 turned hastily away from the lapping water.

The inhabitants of P4V-837—who also did not appear in the M.A.L.P. data—weren't quite human, though they did walk on two legs, have two arms, and heads on top. Bilaterally symmetrical in all respects, they were clothed in something that shimmered and blurred in the yellow sunlight, as if it couldn't quite decide what it wanted to be. As they watched, the material, if it was material, shifted and flowed over the aliens' bodies until it was a reasonable facsimile of the team's fatigues.

"Ooooh-kay," O'Neill muttered.

All three aliens had large brown eyes, but their faces were covered with patterns of hair in different colors, growing in weblike lines. It was difficult to read expressions when five or six eyebrows seemed to radiate from the corners of their lips and fantastic curliques of brown, red, and silver, respectively, decorated their brows.

"Hello?" Daniel said tentatively.

The three aliens looked at each other and then back at the team.

"Hello," they responded.

The members of SG-1 all let go unconsciously held breaths. Once again, the aliens spoke English. It was *such* a convenience when it worked out that way.

"Uh, hi. We come in peace?"

The patterns of hair rippled across the three faces. O'Neill was pretty sure that meant the aliens were laughing at them. "You carry weapons," Silver pointed out.

"You never know when a tree is going to try to eat you," O'Neill muttered.

More writhing hair. One of the three turned away to look at the cottonwoods, and they could see that the hair patterns extended over the back of the skull as well. The patches of bare skin were clearly visible—the hair was at most three-quarters of an inch long on Red, who had, comparatively speaking, the most luxurious mane of the three.

"We carry weapons to protect ourselves, not to attack peaceful people," Daniel continued gamely. "We'd like to be friends."

"We'd like to understand what just happened here," O'Neill added rather waspishly.

"What happened?" The three faced each other again, and O'Neill caught a low mutter among them. Lip reading would be impossible with these guys, he thought, and then brought himself up short. There was no reason to assume they were male, he reminded himself. They might all be Samantha Carters.

In which case it was probably a good thing they weren't all as well armed as Major Carter, who was keeping a solid grip on her rifle, ready to bring it to bear in an instant. Teal'C was somewhat more comfortable with the situation, the butt end of his energy staff firmly grounded on the soft grass.

Brown broke out of the huddle and faced them, his mouth stretching wide as if parodying a smile. "We wish you welcome," he—or she—said. "Wise ones are ready to protect themselves whenever necessary, but we are no threat to you. We too wish to be friends. Come with us."

The three aliens turned and took a few steps away and then looked back expectantly.

The team looked to its leader.

Its leader shrugged. While he'd rather the M.A.L.P. had a chance to get more information about this weird place, the machine couldn't ask questions.

Why not? O'Neill thought, and glanced at his team, gathering their opinions.

The probe had shown a meadow—sans beach— and trees that looked enough like their counterparts on Earth to lead the science team to suspect the flora might have had its origin there. If that was the case, this world was a very hospitable place for Earth species; definitely a keeper. Of course, that was before the current landlords, if that was what they were, showed up. There hadn't been any sign of intelligent life on this world, not even transplanted human beings.

Of course, there hadn't been any video of walking trees and giant parrots, either. Definite oversight on the machine's part.

Daniel was already moving forward. Carter, more suspicious, followed, eyeing the aliens warily. Teal'C exchanged a wordless glance with O'Neill.

Unanimous, then.

SG-1 followed.

The aliens led them through the trees, skipping nimbly over the exposed roots. O'Neill took the opportunity to glance back to the Gate and as a result saw the ocean vanish, as a mirage approached too closely will vanish, to be replaced with more meadow, more grasses and trees. He sniffed deeply, but couldn't detect a lingering aroma of salt and fish and kelp. The beach was gone as if it had never been.

But the laces on his boots were still wet.

It was a pleasant walk, or it would have been if his feet were drier. He hung back to watch Daniel eagerly conversing with the three aliens, gesticulating, nodding, pushing his glasses back up on his nose when they slipped down. Carter and Teal'C had fanned out on either side of O'Neill, neatly flanking their hosts.

The open areas between the trees got smaller and smaller as they went on, until they were spending most of their time in the shade. The trees were no longer cottonwoods, either; there were a few aspens, familiar to O'Neill from innumerable ski weekends in Colorado, and more "other" trees—ones he couldn't identify. He wasn't a botanist, and didn't expect to be able to reel off the names of every plant he encountered, but more and more of the trees looked like they came from a world that featured people with odd patterns of hair on their heads. The branches, for instance: they marched up the trunks in perfectly symmetrical rows, and the bark was bright yellow. It just didn't look like home any more.

Silver looked back at him and the others and waved them up closer as they stepped through yet another small clearing and stopped abruptly, the ground falling away from their feet as if it had been sheared off by a knife. But the grasses still grew down the nearly vertical slope, soft and cushiony.

"Come and eat with us," Silver said.

Something about the invitation reminded O'Neill of pomegranate seeds, though he couldn't remember why. He'd have to ask Daniel, who probably had the reference at his fingertips. He wondered if they were expected to roll down the hill, but the three aliens led them off in another direction, and there before them appeared a long stone stairway laid upon the grass, leading downward. O'Neill could have sworn it hadn't been there fifteen seconds earlier.

But the slabs of rock were solid under his feet, and the steps were sufficiently wide and shallow that he didn't look for a railing. The slope looked steeper than it was, apparently. Or maybe it was just another one of those things.

He was relieved to find that no one was expecting them, and there wasn't a banquet laid out ready for interstellar guests. The conical huts at the foot of the stairs were full of people who were just as surprised to see visitors as their visitors were to see them, and

Brown, Red, and Silver did a lot of talking in that low, muttery whisper before the other aliens were convinced and started pulling dinner together.

"There are no children," Teal'C remarked, studying the ebb and flow of aliens gathering, talking, splitting into smaller groups and then regathering as if they needed to touch each other constantly. "Or at least no smaller individuals."

It was true. All of the aliens were about the same height, perhaps five and half feet tall. Fascinated, the team watched as some of the aliens' clothing changed shape into an approximation of fatigues, while on others, the material, whatever it was, remained static. The uninfluenced version of the clothing appeared to be layers of fabric in panels perhaps a foot wide, hanging from shoulders and hips, fluttering as the aliens moved.

Finally Brown rejoined the Earth team. "Come and eat," he invited. "Share our food."

"You guys go ahead," O'Neill said. "I'll stand watch."

"You're sure?" Jackson asked.

"Oh, yeah, I'm sure."

So the rest of the team settled down on the ground around the gray drop cloths that served as picnic blankets, and O'Neill watched as the aliens brought them apples and bread. No pomegranates, he noted, and wondered why he was obsessing on the subject.